JUST DESSERTS AND MURDER

A TEMPERANCE MATTHEWS COZY MYSTERY

LITTLE BAKERY COZY MYSTERY SERIES

LUCINDA RACE

MC TWO PRESS

Editor NN Light / Blossoming Pages
Cover design by Jacobs Ink
Manufactured in the United States of America
First Edition January 2026

Print Edition ISBN 978-1-966424-43-7
Large Print ISBN 978-1-966424-44-4
Hardcover ISBN 978-1-966424-45-1
E-book ISBN 978-1-966424-42-0

1

QUICK NOTE: If you enjoy Just Desserts & Murder, check out my offer for a FREE novella at the end. With that, happy reading.

I STOOD IN THE COOL, hazy light at sunrise as I watched my dream turn to ash. Firefighters sprayed water on what remained of the Early Rise Bakery. The weak sun painted the horizon a shade of pink that should have inspired a sweet and creamy frosting; instead, a sour taste coated my mouth. *'Up in smoke'* took on an unpleasant, new meaning.

"Temperance?"

I turned. My best friend, Josie Shaw, ran toward me, her arms outstretched. She wrapped me in a bear hug. "I'm so sorry. Why didn't you call me?"

"I wasn't waking anyone in the wee hours of the morning to say my bakery was on fire. It was bad enough I got the call."

She searched my face, but there were no tears; I had cried them out an hour ago. "Do they know what happened?"

Turning my back on the end of a brief career as a baker, I

shook my head. "Not yet. I got here around five and have been watching them get the blaze under control. They'll bring in an arson team to determine what caused the fire." Disbelief washed over me. "I have a checklist which I follow at the end of each day, and I've replayed closing the shop yesterday afternoon a dozen times. I'm positive I didn't leave any equipment on."

Giving me a knowing smile, she looked over my shoulder. "Why are more cops arriving now?"

"They need a couple to stay with the fire department while they continue to wet it down, just in case there's a spark." But as Josie mentioned, several more officers were walking about, and it wasn't time for a shift change.

A tall male officer strode across the street to join the fire chief and a policewoman. They gestured toward the smoldering remains of the building. It was light enough to see the newcomers nod, and they followed the chief to what had been the north side of the structure. Taking a step forward, with Josie beside me, I tracked their movements, wishing I could hear their conversation.

Leaning into me in a whisper, she asked, "What do you think that's all about?"

"I don't know, but it's curious."

They made their way to the back of the building, where an entrance used to be. The chief pointed to something on the ground. The female officer knelt closer. They must be talking; it was hard to see if their mouths were moving from this distance, but the nodding and hand gestures told an important story without words. Something was wrong.

"This isn't good."

I shook my head. "No, and I'd like to know what's happening. I own the building. They should discuss whatever happened with me."

As the words left my mouth, the fire chief pointed to me, and the policeman nodded. "And here we go." I walked north and was going to skirt around the hoses on the ground when a fireman stopped me.

"It's not safe here."

I wish they wore name tags and not badge numbers. "That's my building—what's left of it—and I need to speak with the officers," I said, gesturing to the group heading my way.

"Wait here."

A man of few words.

Josie stood beside me as we waited. My mouth went dry as I observed their grim expressions.

When they reached me, the tall officer said, "Ms. Matthews, I'm Sergeant Franklin. This is your bakery, correct?" Fire Chief Wool and the female officer stood to one side without speaking.

"It was. Does anyone know what happened?" I looked to my friend, the fire chief, Erik Wool.

The Sergeant said, "That's what I was going to ask you. Could you have left a burner on or another small appliance on, like a coffee maker?"

"The coffee pots are on timers and, if empty, shut off after thirty minutes. In addition, I use a checklist when I shut down every day. There's no way I could have left anything on."

He gave a brisk nod. "Do you have staff that comes in late at night to bake?"

"No. I arrive at five, and the two ladies who work for me arrive at six. We prepare most of the dough in the afternoon prior to closing."

He said nothing in response.

"Why do you ask?"

"I'm sorry to inform you, we've discovered a body near the back entrance. It's possible they were overcome by smoke while trying to get out and succumbed. We won't know for sure until the autopsy results are in."

"Sergeant, I locked the store at four o'clock when I left for the day. Nobody should have been in the bakery after that." I pulled out my cell phone. "We can check my camera feeds."

"I'll need access to your footage."

"Consider it done. If you can provide me with an email, I'll send it over as soon as I'm home."

He withdrew a card from his chest pocket. "You can email it here," he said, narrowing his eyes. "Ms. Matthews, I understand your former occupation was as an FBI analyst. Do us both a favor; don't think you can analyze this information. We have experts in the department. Do I make myself clear?"

I shuffled a step back. "Crystal."

The policewoman stepped forward as Sergeant Franklin gestured for Chief Wool to follow him. "I'm Officer Casey Butler. I want to ask you a few questions."

"Of course. Anything I can do to help."

She said, "Let's move out of the way."

Josie and I followed her, glancing over my shoulder to see what else might be happening.

Once we were on the other side of the street on the grassy strip, Officer Butler stopped. She faced the building, and I stood next to her to see what was happening.

"Ms. Matthews, talk to me about yesterday. Were there any unhappy customers or anything out of the ordinary that occurred?"

"It was a typical Friday. We were hectic in the morning. Josie came in to lend a hand since Louise, who usually handles the counter, showed up late."

"Is that unusual?"

"For Josie to lend a hand or Louise's tardiness?"

"Both."

"Yes. Josie's filled in at the bakery as needed."

"Her last name is, and who else works for you?"

Josie said, "My last name is Shaw. I live on Vine Street."

The officer gave Josie an assessing look. "Thank you."

"My employees, Louise Fletcher, she manages the front of house, and Gina Davis, who's the pastry chef—bakes cakes, pies, and specialty items."

Officer Butler nodded. "Have you had problems with either of these women?"

"No. They've worked for me since I opened the bakery eighteen months ago."

"What did you do before moving to town?"

Well, at least she knew I was a recent transplant, and hadn't she heard what the Sergeant said? "My Aunt Penny passed away a little over two years ago and left me her home. It's the Victorian with the bright pink front door and shutters on Mahogany Street."

"I know the place."

"My previous job was stressful, and I needed a change. My dream had been to open a bakery, so I did. I relocated two years ago and bought the bakery. I have a lot of regular customers, and the business has been profitable."

She shot me a sidelong glance as she scribbled a few notes. "What was your job before moving to Oak Hollow?"

My chin dipped. I always hated this part of the conversation since reactions ran the gamut. But I had to respect the officer's questions. "I was an intelligence analyst."

"For the FBI?"

"Yes."

"Hmm." She made another note. "Do you have any known enemies?"

"Not that I'm aware of."

"Anyone who might have been unhappy with your involvement in cases from your time with the bureau?"

"I was behind the scenes and never went into the field. To the world, I was anonymous."

She gave me a piercing stare. Almost as if she didn't believe me. "Were Louise or Gina having any problems with anyone at the bakery or outside of work?"

"I tried to keep things professional. We were friendly, but I didn't know the intimate details of their life." I glanced at the building again. "Do you suspect one of my employees is the victim?"

"What makes you think we found human remains?"

"Sergeant Franklin just said a body was discovered near the back entrance." Was she trying to trip me up by dangling a cookie like I was a pup?

"Right."

The way she elongated a single word was reminiscent of what an agent might do when processing information I had provided, even when it contradicted their expectations. Misleading the witness was a typical tactic and one I didn't appreciate, especially in this situation.

"Do you have any idea who it might be?" I asked.

"Not yet. You'll be informed as soon as we identify the body. However, it would be helpful to have the addresses for your employees."

This was either for a wellness check or to question them. That was easy, I had nothing to hide. I pulled up my contacts in my cell phone and rattled off Louise and Gina's contact information. "Will you need anything else?"

"Not now, except for your and Josie's personal information."

We both gave her the details. "Officer Butler, does the fire chief have a hypothesis about how the fire started?"

Her brow furrowed and her gaze darted to the ash pile. "They used an accelerant."

"Arson?" I clutched Josie's arm as my knees buckled. "Why would anyone want to burn down my bakery?"

"That question needs an answer, along with the victim's name." She snapped her notebook closed and handed me a card. "I'll be in touch, or if you can think of anything else, call me."

I looked around in stunned silence as the sun rays

unveiled the total devastation of what had been my bakery. The structure's cement corners and ghostly shape resembled images I'd seen on the news of fires. I never expected this to happen to me, but I suppose no one ever did.

"At least you have insurance. You can rebuild." Josie wrapped a reassuring arm around my waist to hold me upright on noodle legs.

"True. But what about Louise and Gina? They've lost their jobs, and rebuilding will take months."

"Look at the bright side—you didn't like the layout anyway."

I knew she was trying to be helpful, but it didn't work. The sour taste in my mouth had traveled to my midsection. "My stomach feels like I've been riding an upside-down roller coaster for hours."

"Let me take you home."

I shook my head. "Not yet. A person died in there." Now that the night shadows were gone, I looked up and down South Street. My breath caught, "Josie. Look."

At the end of the street was a bright blue VW convertible. "That's Louise's car." I grabbed her arm and called out for Officer Butler to wait.

She turned around before she reached her squad car. We ran over to her. "The victim might be Louise Fletcher."

"What makes you think that?"

I pointed to the convertible at the corner of South and Mahogany Street. "That's her car."

"Thank you. I'll check it out." She strode across the street.

I looked at Josie, who nodded. We followed her a few steps behind.

"Ms. Matthews, keep your distance."

Although the warning was implied, I still needed to know if the car belonged to Louise. "We won't interfere. I want to help if I can."

The officer attempted to open the car doors but found

them locked. She peered inside, walked around to the back, and pressed the button on her walkie-talkie, reporting the license plate number for a check.

I said, "Louise always kept a spare key in a magnetic case under the back bumper."

"How would you know that?"

"She was always locking herself out. I suggested that as an easy solution, so she did. It saved her from calling Triple A or her boyfriend to unlock the car."

As Officer Butler examined the bumper, my fingers twitched to assist her. "It should be on the driver's side."

She patted under the bumper and withdrew a small metal box. "Is this it?"

I nodded. "Yes."

She said, "Stay here and touch nothing," before striding back to her sedan.

I took the opportunity to glance inside the car. On the back seat lay a duffle bag, a stack of paperback novels, a cooler, a pair of sneakers, flip-flops, hiking boots, and a pink baseball cap with the bakery's name on the front.

Josie asked, "Is she going on vacation?"

"Not that I was aware of. She hadn't asked for time off, but it looks as if she was ready to leave town." I hurried around to the passenger side. Her cell phone was on the driver's side floor. "This is really bad. Her phone is in there."

Josie whistled softly, her face grim. "That was like another appendage for her."

"I know." Stepping back as Officer Butler approached pulling on blue latex gloves. She didn't seem to notice that I had taken a cursory look.

"Stand back, please." Coming around the front of the vehicle, she put the key in the door lock and, using a flashlight, scanned the interior before unlocking it. With the door opened, she checked the glove compartment and scanned a paper she withdrew, folded it up, and replaced it.

I didn't need confirmation. "That's Louise's cell phone on the floor; she'd never leave it behind. It was a part of her."

"Noted." Her radio squawked. "Go ahead."

"Butler, no one is home at the Fletcher residence. The door was locked, but we looked in the windows, and by the state of the bedroom, drawers were opened and closet doors wide; she may have left in a hurry."

Butler turned her back and walked a few steps away. "Fletcher's car is near the scene of the fire. I'll get it towed, and we can examine it for evidence."

"Copy that."

She gave us a sharp look and said, "I hope you're not trying to listen in on a police conversation."

"Not at all, and we didn't hear a thing." I nodded to the fire. "This is overwhelming."

Her face softened. "I'm sorry about your building. We will find who's responsible."

I swallowed hard. It was too bad Louise got caught up in whatever happened here. "I'm confident you will."

Josie said, "It's unfortunate that Louise may have been involved, whether as a victim or participant."

Officer Butler gave her a stern look. "Do you have something to share, Ms. Shaw?

"Nope."

"It's just a logical observation." I snapped my fingers. "Wait. She did argue with someone yesterday; it was before the lunch rush, and she took a call in the storage room."

2

Office Butler crossed her arms. "Tell me anything you might have overheard. My first question is, who was Louise Fletcher talking to?"

"I'm not sure. I didn't go in when I realized she was on the phone."

"You permit your employees to take personal calls while working?"

"We weren't busy, and she's never left customers waiting while she's working. Besides, Josie was there."

"Has anyone been bothering or upsetting her lately, or has she said anything to you about it?"

I shook my head. "She never said a word; it was business as usual in the bakery."

"Would Gina Davis have a better idea about what might have happened in Ms. Fletcher's life?"

I asked, "Are they friends outside of work?"

She nodded, "Yes."

"You'd have to ask Gina. I don't want to speak on her behalf. They were friendly at the bakery if that means anything."

"I'll be questioning Ms. Davis next. If you think of anything that might be useful, you know how to reach me."

She left us standing on the perimeter of the fire hoses. When she was far enough away, I looked at Josie. "Did you notice anything yesterday that, in hindsight, would indicate something was seriously upsetting Louise?"

"Ever since we noticed the car, I've been replaying yesterday as if it's on a loop. When she left the storage room, her face was beet red, and her eyes were hard. She was efficient with customers but not her usual friendly self."

"So, she was angry. The call had upset her." That was intriguing. At least she didn't let it show to customers, not that it mattered now. The poor woman was presumed dead. I shoved my hands into my jacket pockets. "Josie, do you think Louise and Gina are good friends?"

"They might hang out, but I'm not aware that they're best friends, and I've never seen them around town together. Why? Do you think Gina has information that could help the police uncover what happened?"

"Someone does." The fire chief was coming toward us.

"Temperance."

I offered him a strained smile. "Erik, do you have any news?"

"Josie, do you know Erik Wool? He was at my picnic a couple of weeks ago, but I'm not sure if you had the chance to talk."

Flashing him a broad smile, she said, "Josie Shaw."

"Erik Wool," he nodded with a smile. "Temperance, I wanted to bring you up to date. We'll be here for a while longer to ensure there are no hot spots, and the winds are expected to increase, so we want to avoid a flare-up. The fire marshal will arrive later this morning to investigate. Make sure to contact your insurance company to start the claim."

His efficiency was appreciated. "I will. Do you have any idea what could have started the fire?"

"In this job, I try to avoid speculation. However, my instinct tells me it's arson." He lowered his head. "I'm sorry for everything. I loved your bakery. Hopefully, the rebuilding won't take long."

"Thanks, Erik. Would it be all right if I baked some cookies or muffins and dropped them at the firehouse? I'd like to thank the men and women who tried to save my business."

"That'd be great. They love to eat, and we never turn down donations of great food." He touched my arm. "Again, I'm real sorry."

"Will someone keep me informed on the investigation?"

"You can check with Casey Butler. She's been on the scene today and is one of the best in the department."

"Is she new? I don't recall seeing her in my bakery."

"For about a year, but she works the night shift so that she wouldn't have stopped in for a coffee. Unlike the day shift cops."

Nodding, I said, "Good to know."

His radio crackled. "Chief? A word."

"Copy that." He nodded at the small group of firefighters gathered near the ladder truck. "I need to go. We'll talk later." He jogged over the hoses and joined them.

"This isn't the right time, but," Josie said, "he's cute. Did you see those blue eyes? Yummy."

Laughing, I poked her in the shoulder. "Only you could see beyond the soot and grime. Also, I'm not sure if you noticed him at the picnic, but he was there alone."

She glanced his way, and her eyes twinkled. "Good to know! I noticed him, but you know me; I see a handsome man, and my tongue gets twisted. Besides, his interest might lie elsewhere."

"I've never seen him with anyone." I withdrew my cell phone from my jacket and took pictures of the destruction and the onlookers. I had countless questions, and now that it was morning, many curiosity seekers gathered. Perhaps someone in the crowd was admiring their handiwork.

Josie watched as I rotated in a one-eighty pattern, taking more pictures. I turned back, selected the video option, and moved in slow motion to capture everything that was happening.

As she stepped closer, she asked, "What are you thinking?"

"Someone in this crowd knows something. If I can examine the images, there may be a clue that I can share with the police."

Her brow quirked. "Is this where your former profession will come in handy?"

"Analyzing data for potential threats won't work, but dissecting a pattern might. If this were arson, all perps have a signature. To be honest, a part of me hopes it is. I wouldn't want the reason someone perished inside my bakery be due to faulty wiring or another issue I could have prevented."

"Whatever happened, *you* are not to blame."

Her words were comforting, but my insides felt hollow. *How could this be happening to me?* "Do you see that couple hovering near the post office? From this angle, I can't make out who they are."

"The couple wearing straw fedoras?"

"That's them. Do you recognize who they are?"

"They look familiar. I might have seen them around town. But I'd need a closer look to be sure."

I held up my phone and took a series of pictures of the couple, suspects one and two, before handing my cell to her. "Have a look. We can blow up the images later for a positive identification," I said.

She enlarged the picture and laughed. "No need; it's Jonah and Celeste. I see many regulars from the bakery watching the tragedy unfold."

Nodding, I said, "What are they doing dressed like that? Trying to disguise who they are?"

She shook her head. "Who knows, but here comes one of your regulars now."

"Temperance." Russ Patterson held his hard hat under his arm as he pulled me in for a hug. His brown eyes clouded with concern. "This is terrible. I was coming in for my usual and was shocked to see the devastation. I heard it might be arson?"

"At this stage, anything is possible."

"If you need anything, just let me know. Here's my number. I'm happy to have a crew clear the debris once the scene is released."

"Thanks. That's very kind of you."

"Unfortunately, it's gas station coffee for me today," he said, nodding to Josie. "Keep an eye on Temperance."

"Will do."

"Have a good day, Russ." He strode down the street and got in his truck. Our eyes met briefly. "If the worst part of his day is drinking terrible coffee, he should consider himself lucky."

Josie chuckled. "I thought the same thing." She turned to face me. "Do you see that short woman wearing a pink raincoat and a hat pulled low to cover her face standing in front of Ruggles Cheese?"

I looked around her. "Yes, isn't that Alice?"

"It is. Yesterday at the bakery, she grilled Louise about the day-old bread and muffins, questioning her repeatedly if they were just a day old and not multiple days sitting on the rack."

"Was that before or after the lunch rush?"

"Afterward. She comes in all the time and always buys day-old items. So, it's odd that she was challenging Louise about them."

"Louise knows I throw away anything left over from that

shelf at the end of the day. Unless Mic is coming into town, he'll call and ask me to put it out back for his pigs."

"It was strange. However, Alice bought a large box of assorted muffins and rolls and stormed out in a huff."

I took a couple of pictures of suspect number one since I didn't consider Jonah and Celeste would be involved. "Do you think Gina might be a suspect?"

"Rut roh. Look out, our friendly Officer Butler is coming over."

I loved the Scooby Doo reference. "Any news?"

She frowned. "Are you photographing the crowd?"

"Yes, I thought they could be valuable if my insurance company requested documentation." I looked her in the eyes. "Is that a problem?"

"Is that your only reason? Sergeant Franklin isn't happy with what you might be doing."

"Watching my dream literally go up in smoke, I'm left wondering what I should do next. Rest assured, I'm not doing anything I shouldn't."

Placing her hands on her belt, she squared her stance. "Going home is a better idea. Leave this investigation to the professionals, it's in your best interest. Also, no more pictures."

The force behind her words didn't deter me. "What makes you think I'm…"

"Look. I don't care that you're taking pictures. It's odd, but whatever. However, if the killer and arsonist are watching the scene and see you poking around, they might feel threatened and come after you next. I don't think that will happen, but for your safety, stop."

I held up my hands in surrender. "Fine. I won't take any more pictures, but you should know that the woman in the pink raincoat, in front of the cheese shop? That's Alice. Josie saw her arguing with Louise at the bakery." Yesterday felt like a lifetime ago or like I was in the Twilight Zone.

She pivoted and looked toward Ruggles. "Does Alice have a last name?"

"I can't remember." I pinched the bridge of my nose and took a breath.

"Wait, it's Sullivan," Josie nodded.

"A few weeks ago she came to a picnic at my place with Peter Swanson."

"Anything else you want to share based on your observations?"

I shook my head, then Josie said, "There's Jonah and Celeste, also known as Straw-Hat Fedora Man and Lady. They've been attentive to what's happening and were customers at the bakery yesterday."

"They're regulars and harmless. I bought the business from them."

"I'm sure nearly everyone in town, except for me, has been to Early Rise." Her voice sounded flat. "I'll look into these people for alibis."

She should have referred to them as suspects, but I'd let it go for now. Everyone was in *my* line of suspicion, and I'd do some digging. Even if I didn't have the connections I once had when I was with the FBI, my brain still functioned. "Thank you for everything."

"You're welcome." Giving me a brisk nod, Officer Butler made her way to Alice. This could be interesting to witness.

"Josie, should we hang out?" I darted my eyes toward Officer Butler and Alice.

"Heck yeah, I don't have much else going on this morning, and I'm curious to see if she talks to Jonah and Celeste as well."

"Don't you have work?"

"My transcription projects have dried up for the moment. I'm in a holding pattern until day after tomorrow, so I'm free as a bird for the next forty-eight hours."

The corners of my lips dipped. "Me too. What do you

want to do? We could go to my house for breakfast?" The group of onlookers slowly dispersed. Now that the fire was out and some firemen were rolling up hoses, people seemed to lose interest.

"Don't you need to make some calls? Vendors, insurance people, and I'm not sure who else."

I nodded. "That can wait for a bit. I'll fix breakfast, and while we eat, I can compile a list of everything that needs to be done: cancel food orders, contact the insurance company, and talk with Gina."

"Breakfast sounds great, and I'll do anything to help." She turned slowly in a circle. "I wonder why she isn't in the crowd."

"Who knows? She didn't want to confront the pain of losing her job." Guilt twisted in my stomach, wondering how Gina could react when she learned about Louise.

Josie slipped her arm around my shoulder. "You're under no obligation to tell Gina about Louise. I'm sure Officer Butler will inform her when she questions her."

A wave of relief washed over me. Confessing the truth to Josie was unthinkable—I couldn't face Gina, and I didn't want to be alone right now. My business was gone, and it seemed an employee had lost their life in the fire. "How long do you think it takes to construct a building?"

"Six months or more. Consider how long it takes to build a house. Unfortunately, you're starting from worse than scratch. You'll need to wait for the area to be cleared, which happens after the investigation is closed. It may be closer to nine months. What do you think you'll do in the meantime?"

My heart sank a little lower in my chest. All I wanted to do was bake—breads, cakes, muffins, and cookies. Toss in the occasional pie, and I was in heaven. It's why I left the bureau, to make a difference in people's lives one loaf of bread at a time. "For the record, I make great bread."

Josie laughed. "Did I miss part of the conversation?"

"Just the one in my head. I was thinking about why I moved here and opened the bakery. Spending summers here was the best part of my childhood, and when Aunt Penny left me her house, it was the push I needed to change my life. Being a city girl wasn't for me anymore, and after everything I witnessed…" A shiver raced over me. I rubbed my arms to get some warmth back into them.

She steered us toward Mahogany Street. "A walk will do us both good. It'll clear the smoke from our nostrils, and we can enjoy the sunshine."

"Temperance! Wait!"

I froze when I heard my name. "Gina?"

She ran down the street, weaving around bystanders, and skidded to a stop in front of us. Her breath came in heaving gulps. "Temperance. Is it true?"

Pointing to what remained of the bakery, I said, "The fire? Yes."

She dropped her hands to her knees, sucking in deep breaths.

"Did you run from your house?"

"The police came. Told me about. Louise. I left. Ran here."

I rubbed her back. "Slow down. Catch your breath, and we'll talk." I guided her to a bench in front of the bank. Josie sat on one side, and I was on the other.

Withdrawing an inhaler, she took two puffs. Gradually, her breathing returned to normal, and she looked up; her skin was blotchy, and tears dampened her face. Was it from the shock or the all-out run? That remained to be seen. "Is it true? Louise is dead?"

"We're not sure yet, but a body was discovered near the bakery door. The identity has yet to be confirmed. However, Louise's car is down the street, and the back seat contains a duffel bag and other items. It seems she was planning to leave town."

"She's not. Her boyfriend kicked her out of their house.

Remember, yesterday, she was very upset right before noon?"

Ah, the phone call in the storage room. "Yes."

"That jerk called her during a shift and broke it off. He told her he'd put her things on the porch, and she could pick them up after work. She was frantic, and until she found a place, she was going to live out of her car. I offered her my couch, but she said she wasn't looking for charity and would find a new place, even if it was just a single room."

"I wish I'd known. She could have stayed with me until she found a place."

"She'd never have taken you up on it, and now..." Gina dropped her head into her hands, her breath started coming in short, quick spurts. She withdrew the inhaler from her pocket and took another puff.

My eyes widened as I looked at Josie over her head. How could I have missed all of that happening right under my nose? What kind of boss was I?

"Gina, I'm sorry that all this happened. Do you think her boyfriend might have harmed her?"

Her head snapped up. "Wasn't kicking her out enough? I bet she snuck into the bakery to use the restroom and..." She wiped her damp cheeks. "You know."

I nodded. She didn't need to say what was on our minds. "Josie, will you stay with Gina while I speak with Officer Butler?"

"Of course."

As I scanned the scene. I raised a hand to signal the officer. She nodded and gestured for me to come over.

When I reached her, I gestured to Gina. "I learned some interesting information. Gina mentioned that Louise's boyfriend kicked her out of their place, and as of last night, she was living in her car."

"That puts the boyfriend at the top of my suspect list."

I nodded. "Mine too."

3

—————

Josie and I sat on the front porch with mugs of coffee, sipping in silence as we gazed across the street at the nature preserve. My mini black and tan dachshund, Hank, was curled up on my lap, snoring softly.

I should be in the bakery pulling pans of crusty bread out, not waiting for the oven bell to ding in my home kitchen for baked French toast. "I felt terrible when Gina told us about Louise and her boyfriend. He was at the party; what was your impression of them? Did you think they were unhappy?"

"They were opposites in every way. Marty's short, maybe five-foot-six, with blond hair, brown eyes, and very thin. He looked like a stiff wind would knock him over. I wouldn't have pegged them as a couple, if you know what I mean."

Closing my eyes, I said, "She was vivacious, about the same height as Marty but with curves, with dark hair and soft green eyes, and her laugh—heavens, I'm going to miss that sound." Tears sprang to my eyes, and I blinked them back.

"Is her family local?"

I shook my head. "Not that I'm aware of. I wish I had

gotten to know her better. Maybe if she were in trouble, I could have helped."

Josie shot a glance in my direction and locked eyes with me. "Stop chastising yourself."

This helpless feeling overwhelmed my emotions. "What do you want me to do? My stomach is in knots."

Leaning forward, she tapped my knee, drawing my gaze to hers. "Don't all crimes have a pattern? Tells, a signature? You mentioned it before. Focus on that."

Before answering, I contemplated her question. "It's true that crimes can involve elements of randomness. Not every crime is a copycat of others. Patterns exist in timing, location, and even in people's behavior. Events in the offender's life may seem benign at first glance, but when viewed as a whole, patterns emerge."

"Like, a bank robber doesn't start with the big heist," she said.

"Correct. It's typical they start shoplifting at a much younger age, either for the thrill or the need. Some shoplifters steal necessities, when someone is hungry they might steal food. Over time, and without proper intervention, this behavior evolves into stealing larger or more expensive items, until they establish a pattern of what they steal and why."

"Did you do this in your previous job?"

"Yes. If you can understand the pattern, you can predict the next series of moves."

With eyes wide, she asked, "You were a profiler?"

"No." I stood, holding Hank in my arms, crossed to the porch railing, and leaned against it with my back to the puffs of smoke. "I dealt less with the offender's psychology and more with the data regarding where a series of crimes might occur. However, the two departments worked closely together, so I understand the basics."

Ding. "That's breakfast. I'll be right back with plates."

She stood, and I placed my hand on her shoulder. "Relax. I've got this."

I entered the oversized kitchen and sighed before placing Hank on his cushy bed in the corner. I loved this room, it featured ample counter space, a commercial range and refrigerator, and an extra set of double ovens. When Aunt Penny renovated the kitchen, she dreamed of opening a bed and breakfast, but later after her first weekend guests, she decided she didn't want to cater to demanding visitors. In this space, I had perfected my bread and biscuit-making, and my chocolate cookie recipe. Pressing my hand to my heart, I stifled the sob that threatened to escape.

"What am I going to do now?" The memory of Aunt Penny standing next to me as I cut butter into flour for the biscuits, encouraging me as I rolled out the dough, and her words, *'Don't give up, Tempie, roll up your sleeves and keep going. If this batch doesn't work, we'll feed the birds and try again.'* Her approach was to keep at it and not let a setback derail you. Despite the heaviness in my chest, I smiled. Maybe for today, I'd wallow—just a little.

I plated breakfast for two, adding berries, a sliced banana, and a small pitcher of maple syrup, then returned the baking dish to the oven in case we wanted seconds. Leaving the pup inside, I pushed open the screen door and stepped onto the porch. My mouth gaped; I would have dropped the tray if I hadn't had a firm grasp on it.

A woman stumbled up the path. "Louise?"

Josie jumped to her feet. "We thought you were dead."

Louise, her hair spiked in places with twigs sticking out, her jacket torn, and missing a shoe. "Temperance. Help me." She collapsed onto the ground.

I set the tray aside. Josie and I rushed down the stairs. I dropped to my knees. "Josie, call the police. Tell them Louise Fletcher is lying on my walkway and needs medical assistance." I pressed my fingers to the underside of her wrist, and the beat was steady. That was a good thing.

"Hi, this is Josie Shaw. I'm at Temperance Matthews's home at 110 Mahogany Street. We found Louise Fletcher, nearly unconscious, on Temperance's walkway; we believe she was in the rubble from the bakery fire, but she's alive. Please send the police and an ambulance. "

Rubbing her hand gently, I leaned in closer. "Louise, come on sweetie, open your eyes. Help is on the way."

It seemed she was in a stupor. I continued rubbing her chilled hands. The sound of a police cruiser grew closer, and the ambulance would soon follow.

Her eyes stayed closed as she let out a soft groan. I wanted to lift her up but understood that it was important not to move someone who had collapsed, in case they had more serious injuries that weren't visible. Who knows where she had been or what had happened to her since she left her car?

Tires chipped at the curb. I looked up. Officer Butler jogged over. "What's happened?"

"Louise Fletcher stumbled up the walk, asked for help, and collapsed."

"Was anyone with her?"

"Not that I saw. I'd been in the house, came out with breakfast, and she was standing there. Josie was on the porch. I think we saw Louise at the same time."

The ambulance came to a stop, then the driver and passenger doors opened as the EMTs moved to the back of the vehicle. Moments later, they approached us.

"Temperance, can you step back?"

Relief washed over me as I saw Van Jonas and Dave Buckle, whom I had come to know during my summers here. Louise was in excellent hands.

Van wrapped a blood pressure cuff around Louise's upper arm and looked up. "Do you know if she takes any medications?"

"Not that I know of."

"Any health issues?"

I shook my head. "Again, no."

She squeezed her eyes tighter and gasped, "Type One."

Dave pulled out a small test kit. "I'm going to test her blood sugar."

He poked her index finger and looked at the meter. "Louise, your blood sugar is extremely high. We'll give you something to help stabilize it and then transport you to the hospital. Are you hurt anywhere else?"

"No. Insulin in my cooler."

"We have everything under control. Just take it easy; we'll sit you up and give you some glucose gel. You'll be just fine." Dave glanced at Van.

"Officer Butler, can you help Van with the gurney?"

"Yes."

The look between Dave and Van was grim. How long had she been without her medication? It looked like she had been wandering in the woods all night. Officer Butler and Van were back quickly. Once Louise was half-sitting on the gurney, Dave gave her the gel.

"I'll help you squeeze this between your teeth and cheek. We'll wait a bit and then recheck your numbers."

"So thirsty."

"We'll get you something to drink once we arrive at the emergency room. The doctor should examine you first."

With a slight nod, she said, "Boss, could you call Gina and ask her to meet me at the hospital?"

"Of course. Would you like me to come too?"

"I'll be fine. You need to get to work."

A puzzled look washed over my face as I glanced at the officer and then Josie. I mouthed. *Doesn't she know about the fire?*

Bobbing my head toward the porch, Officer Butler followed me up. Josie held Louise's hand.

She asked, "What else can you tell me?"

"Nothing. If she's here, then who's the victim in my bakery?"

"That's an interesting question. Any hypothesis?"

I shook my head. "Not a single one. Is it okay if I inform Gina about what has happened?"

"Yes. I assume they will admit Louise for observation. Once she's stable, I can question her about last night."

"Maybe she witnessed something at the bakery, got scared, and fled into Green Stride Wood for safety."

"It's possible. I'm unfamiliar with the layout. What can you tell me?"

"Not much. It's a protected area due to its turtle habitat. There's a Miller's Pond half a mile back and some walking trails. Hank and I take walks in there almost daily. At the pond, there's a small clearing with tables and benches for people to picnic. The side of my property borders the area, as it does on the opposite side of the street. Louise could have walked through the woods and ended up here."

"Could she have camped there for the night?"

"No, it's carry-in and carry-out only, sunrise to sunset. This doesn't mean that teenagers don't go out to the pond after dark, but it's posted. I noticed her shoe is missing, her jacket's torn, and twigs are stuck in her hair. This wasn't a casual stroll."

She raised an eyebrow. "Do you always pay attention to every little detail?"

I smiled slightly. "Isn't that what you expected from me? You're asking me to share my observations. If I don't tell you what I notice, there's a chance you might overlook something important. You can't monitor everything and everyone all the time."

"True, but Temperance, you aren't a police officer. I don't want you to get caught up in the crossfire with a murderer."

"I appreciate your concern. I have skills that are valuable

in this situation." I didn't mention that we switched from Ms. to my first name.

"You can call Gina." She walked across the porch and paused before continuing down the steps. "I'm not encouraging you, but if you see or hear anything, let me know." She marched down the steps without looking back.

My lips twitched. I was getting under that crusty exterior. Progress.

I called Gina and waited for her to pick up. I heard, "Hello."

"Hi, Gina. This is Temperance. Can you sit down? I have news."

"What happened?" I noticed the tremor in her voice.

"It's all good. Louise is alive, and she's being transported by ambulance to the emergency room. She's asking for you. Could you meet her there?"

"Louise? Alive?"

I smiled. "Yes, aside from a few scratches and her insulin being out of balance, I believe she's unharmed."

"That is the best news! Where was she, how's her sugar numbers, and why was her car parked near the bakery?"

"I don't have any answers, but will you meet her? She's asking for you."

"Yes! I can be there in twenty minutes. Sooner if I speed."

I said, "Please, keep to the posted limits. She'll be thrilled to see a friendly face."

"Thanks for calling, Temperance."

"Please do me a favor and keep me updated on how she's doing."

"Consider you in the loop. I gotta get dressed so I can be there for her."

"Drive safely." But my words fell on deaf ears, as she had already disconnected.

The ambulance pulled away from the curb, and Officer

Butler, whom I had started to think of as Casey, headed in the opposite direction. Perhaps she was going to the station since it was past eight, and I was sure her shift had ended. Josie sank down onto the porch step.

"Breakfast? There's more warming in the oven."

"Maybe I'll have a fresh mug of coffee first, but I'm starved."

I smiled. "Inside or out?"

"Let's try this again. Despite everything that has occurred, dining al fresco remains a wonderful idea on a sunny morning."

"Give me a hand," I said, holding open the screen as we walked in. Hank lifted his sleepy head, then lay back down, stretched out, and yawned. Such is the life of a pup.

"Could the last few hours have been any weirder?"

I wished I could laugh, but the issue of who had been in my bakery still weighed on my mind. "I can't stop thinking about who the firemen found, if it's not Louise. Don't get me wrong; I'm thrilled she's safe. We know Gina's fine, so who was in the store, and what the heck happened? Is Oak Hollow PD capable of discovering the truth?"

"Officer Butler asked me if I had seen anything before Louise came up the walk, but I hadn't. I trust she won't give up until they figure this out. The truth will rise, even if they need to call for reinforcements."

Now I smiled. "A yeast pun?"

"It made you smile, and if you don't enjoy your breakfast, I'll continue with the puns."

I slid the dish from the oven. "Josie, what's going to happen next? This has been a roller coaster since three this morning when I got the call about the fire. By the time I arrived fifteen minutes later, it was an inferno. They could only keep dousing the real estate office to prevent it from meeting the same fate."

"I can't imagine what it was like to watch the fire. It was bad enough after I got there and saw for myself. On a positive note, you were on a corner with a wide alley separating you and the other buildings."

Tilting my head, I said, "I've been thinking about this, and trust me, I'm not an expert in fires, but if the blaze started in the early morning hours, aside from the gas lines, which, thankfully, didn't rupture, I don't have many fuel sources inside the building. Most surfaces are metal. And why didn't the gas lines explode?"

"Could someone have shut it off?"

I could feel the cogs of my brain kick into gear. "Someone must have turned off the gas before starting the fire. Next, find out who in town knows how to shut off the gas supply. Third, obtain a copy of the report on the fire."

"Wouldn't nearly everyone in town know how to turn off a gas main?"

I served her a plate of hot French toast. "Do you know how to turn off your connection?"

A glimmer sparked in her gray eyes. "I don't. Do you?"

"It never even crossed my mind to ask the question until I bought the bakery."

Ruff, ruff. Hank danced around my feet begging for a treat. I took the small canister of pup cookies, with HANK in bold letters, to the table, and he trotted along behind me. With a point of my finger, his little butt hit the floor next to my chair, and his reward was a couple of cookies. He glanced at my plate as if he wanted some of that too.

"Not happening, little boy. It's your cookies or nothing."

He scarfed them down and trotted back to his bed while keeping his eyes trained on me after he settled in. I laughed. "I'm under surveillance." I smacked my hand on the table.

"Josie, how could I be so forgetful? I can check the cameras at the bakery to see how the fire started."

Hank barked his approval, and I gave him another cookie. "Thanks to you, I know what to do next."

4

$\mathcal{I}$ walked into my office off the living room, grabbed my laptop, and hurried back to the kitchen. By the time I returned, Josie had refilled our coffee mugs, and Hank was in her lap.

"I can't believe I didn't think of this as soon as we got back."

"Give yourself a break. A lot has happened, and discovering that Louise might be dead and then alive added an unexpected twist to the morning, in the best way possible, of course."

I entered my password and waited a moment for it to boot up. "You're right. I'm still surprised that Casey Butler didn't push for more details when she was here."

"The officer has had a long night as well. I'm sure this is perplexing even for a professional. Murder doesn't happen in Oak Hollow."

Reluctant to burst her naïve outlook, I let the comment slide. Once my security account loaded, I clicked the history button, starting at midnight, and let it roll at quadruple time, the time stamp of two-fifteen.

I rotated the screen so that Josie could see it. "Two sets of eyes are better than one."

"What am I searching for?" She peered at the screen.

"Movement, people, shadows. We need to note when someone turned off the gas to the building. That's the crucial first step for whoever started the fire."

"Would they have done that first?"

I blew on my coffee and took a sip. "It's logical." I set the playback speed to two times, knowing I could rewind and check again if anything was out of place.

The clock in the footage slipped by until it reached two forty-five. "Look. Right there." I hit the pause button. "Do you see that creeping shadow? It's a person skulking along the back of the building."

"They're moving at a turtle's pace."

I glanced her way. "Stealth mode. The police rarely enter the alley, so whoever this is must not have watched my shop before; otherwise, they would have known it was relatively safe."

"Even if they were aware, someone could have reported a prowler."

Nodding, I replied, "True."

I advance the video in real time. "Once we've watched it, I'll make a copy and send it to the police."

"Will you edit it?"

"Are you asking if I'll only send the clips from two a.m. onward? No, they'll receive all the footage from midnight until the fire department arrives. If they request more, I can send that as well."

She pointed at the shadow. "Is he carrying a tool?"

"It's difficult to say, but given that he went directly to the location of the gas main, I would guess it's a wrench."

"You know a lot about gas mains."

"One thing I've learned in life is the importance of taking safety precautions. For me, I'm terrified of fire, so when I purchased the building, understanding how to turn off the gas was crucial. Not that I ever expected to do it; if there had been a leak, I would have called emergency dispatch for the gas company."

"That makes sense."

My voice rose. "Look right there. A small beam of light. He's making sure the lever is perpendicular to the fitting. He shut it off. Whoever this is, he's the arsonist."

"How can we identify him if we can't see his face?"

"Look at how he's crouched next to the building. We can gauge his height by measuring the length of his limbs. Despite his black clothing, a computer can extract this information and provide us with an accurate estimate." I enlarged the video image.

"He appears slim. Notice how his sweatshirt drapes forward as he leans."

I flashed her a broad smile. "Excellent observation." I fast-forwarded to his next action—opening the back door. "That's odd." I rewound the footage and watched it again. "He didn't force the door open. Could he have had a key?"

"How many people have keys to the bakery?"

"I have four master keys that unlock both the front and back doors: one on my key ring, one hanging next to my back entrance, and one in the safe. You have a master key, as do Gina and Louise, but those keys only open the front door."

I jumped to my feet and rushed to where the pink key should be hanging on the rack. "It's gone."

Josie dumped her bag on the table. Her face paled. "Mine's gone too." She pushed the scattered contents around again. "Wait, I found it."

The discovery of the missing key weighed heavily on my shoulders. "That's a twist I didn't see coming. My spare key was used to gain access to the building."

She swept her purse contents into the bag and set it aside. "Do you have any idea who might have taken it?"

I sank into the chair. "No, it's not like I check daily to see if it's there."

"Think," she urged. "When was the last time you *know* you saw the key on the hook?"

Pressing my fingers to my eyes, I shook my head. "I'm not sure. Maybe it was before the barbecue."

"That was three weeks ago."

Tapping my fingers, I said, "It wasn't a big party; there were Gina and Louise, who brought Marty, Alice, and Peter. Then you, Jonah, Celeste, and Erik Wool. That's when someone must have taken it." Ice water coursed through my veins. "Whoever burned down my bakery was in my home, pretending to be my friend."

She placed her hand over mine. "What's the statistic for crimes committed by a known individual against the victim?"

"I'm not certain of the exact number, perhaps up to fifty percent of the time, and fires are typically set by juveniles. However, at my party, there were couples and singles, so I'm going to rule kids out. I think it's a safe bet that this wasn't a random act."

Her facial features drooped as she sighed. "That's terrifying. To think that one of our friends stole and intentionally set a fire."

"What motivated this? Understanding the reason could clarify the identities of both the victim and the perpetrator."

"In movies or on television, the cops ask the victim whether they have any enemies."

I shook my head. "No one comes to mind. Townspeople seem happy the bakery is thriving."

"Have you checked your email?"

After witnessing the suspect gain access repeatedly, I paused the video footage. "I can check junk mail, but I haven't noticed anything."

I clicked on my email box and skimmed the main area and junk folder. "Nothing." I stared out the window overlooking the backyard. "I can't accept this fire was about me. It was a means to hurt someone else, or it was a senseless act of violence."

"How often does an arsonist turn off a gas main?"

"If this person had been looking for the biggest bang for the torch, they wouldn't have."

A faint smile spread across Josie's face. "Bang. Torch. Nice."

"If I didn't make light of this, I'd cry, and who knows if I could stop." I returned to the footage and hit play again, checking the time stamp. It was now three a.m. "Our guy is inside. I would suspect he is laying out materials to burn, such as cake boxes, drink trays, and the like. It's logical; he didn't bring anything in, and there aren't many potential accelerants."

Pointing to the screen, she said, "Hold up a minute. Who's that?"

A person, who seemed to be roughly the same size as the first, based on their height, slid along the building, approached the door, paused, opened it and then slipped inside. "Two people are in the building."

Josie picked up her cell.

"What are you doing?"

She glanced up. "Neither person brought any flammable substances, so how did the fire get out of control so quickly?"

I raised an eyebrow. "I'm not sure. The items I mentioned would catch fire, but they'd need more accelerant."

"Correct. I'm checking which items in a bakery are flammable." Her eyes widened. "Holy cannoli. Six household items are off the charts: powdered sugar, flour, spices, oils, hand sanitizers, and canned cooking sprays, which you might occasionally use, are extremely flammable and could explode."

"That's not good news." A knot twisted in my gut. "My

bakery is an explosion waiting to happen. I never considered any of those items to be dangerous."

"Why would you? These are all standard items for your business. I'm sorry; I've just made this entire situation more difficult for you."

I got up and paced the length of the kitchen and back, taking deep, cleansing breaths, putting myself in the mindset of those who had broken in. "Person one had a key and planned the fire." When they snuck in, they were alone. But less than a half hour later, person two arrived on the scene. Without hesitation, this person entered the unlocked bakery. How did they know the door was unlocked and had they planned to meet up?

"We should watch the rest of the video to find out what comes next."

I sat down and pressed the playback button. At normal speed, the next fifteen minutes dragged on. The back door opened briefly before closing again.

"What's happening in there? I wish it had sound. Or better yet, cameras inside." A beam of light bounced across the eyebrow windows in the storeroom. "I'll bet this is when they're adding to the fire pile, but they haven't lit it yet."

She glanced at me, and I shrugged. "A logical assumption. Once the fire starts, people will leave."

"We're looking for two people now." The color drained from her face, "Oh, wait. Only one leaves."

I took her hand and gave it a reassuring squeeze. "Remember, this footage is more than six hours old. There's nothing we can do about the past."

She blinked away her tears. "It's agonizing to watch." After pushing back her chair, she placed Hank in his bed and walked over to the coffee pot. "Refill?"

"Please." I continued to observe the events unfolding before my eyes. The back door opened once more, and this time, I noticed a gloved hand and part of the lower arm holding it open. "Now what's happening?" The door closed. This was frustrating. Yet, I took another deep breath. I needed to view all the footage to understand better what occurred so the clues would percolate.

Ten minutes passed when the door burst open. A figure emerged and hurled what I guessed to be the wrench against the building. An orange glow flickered briefly before the door slammed shut. He glanced left and right before running down the alley between the bakery and the real estate office, vanishing from sight.

"The fire's burning." I wanted to turn it off, but like driving past a car accident, I couldn't look away. "Come on, get out of the building."

"Temperance. Maybe we should stop watching. We already know the ending."

"It took ninety minutes for my building to become a total loss. How is that possible?" The sob I had suppressed for the last few hours rushed out. Josie wrapped her arms around me, and I cried. Hank pressed his nose against my leg. The sweet boy wanted to comfort me. I picked him up and held him close after turning the laptop screen away; I couldn't watch anymore. It was soul-crushing.

After crying into Hank's fur, I kissed his head and gently placed him on the floor. "I could spend the day crying, but there are so many questions that spring to mind."

She nodded. "Louise Fletcher. How did she go from work to packing her car with her belongings, to wandering in the woods and almost slipping into a diabetic coma?"

"We need to talk to Marty Thomas."

"Should we let him know about Louise? Maybe he'll feel sorry for her, and she could have a place to stay until she gets back on her feet. After all, they shared a home." Josie tipped her head. "Do you think it's odd Louise didn't ask us to contact Marty? She asked for Gina."

"Not really. They had broken up. I'm sure she's hurting." My stomach grumbled. "First food, then we'll talk to Marty. No matter what Gina said, he seems to be a decent sort of guy."

"You need to put a list together for the police of everyone at your party—one of them took your key."

"Good point. The more information I can provide to the cops, the faster this case might be closed."

Sliding my computer to a spot where I could work, I said, "Thanks for hanging out with me."

"No problem. You work for a while, and I'll fix lunch when you're done. Then we can stop by the police station first and track down Marty second. We should also check with Gina to see how Louise is doing. Maybe once she feels better, she'll be able to answer the burning question: how did she end up wandering in the preserve overnight?"

Having specific tasks made it easier to stay unemotional. My phone rang. "It's Gina."

Josie scraped the plates clean of the congealed remnants from two previous breakfast attempts.

I picked up the phone. "Hi Gina, Josie is with me, and I have you on speaker."

"Hello. I wanted to give you a quick update on Louise. The good news is that she's receiving fluids, and her blood sugar has stabilized. She ate a nutritious breakfast, and we expect for her to be released from the hospital later today. They'll keep her in the emergency room a bit longer just to be sure."

"That's great news!" I gave Josie a thumbs up. "Is she returning to her place?"

"Not today. I know she's eager to talk to Marty and clear the air, but she'll stay at my place tonight so she can get some rest before facing the jerk."

"What about her car? When we saw it on the street, it had

a duffel bag, books, shoes, a cooler, and her cell phone. I'm assuming she kept her insulin in the cooler."

"She does, and she found her car keys in her pocket. That's one reason I'm calling."

"Oh?"

"Boss, I know you have a lot on your plate, but could you swing by once we get back to my place, grab the keys, and drive her car over? If it's too much to ask, never mind; however, since you ladies know the situation, I wouldn't need to explain everything."

"We're happy to help. Message us when you leave the hospital, and we'll come by. We'd love to see her, too."

Josie nodded.

Gina asked, "Is there any news about the fire?"

"Nothing yet. However, I didn't expect to hear anything this soon. The fire marshal needs to conduct his investigation, and, of course, they need to sift through the scene for evidence."

"What will they look for?"

"How the fire started, the types of accelerants used, that kind of thing." I didn't mention anything about the gas main; that shouldn't be common knowledge.

"What about the body? Will they know who it is yet?"

"I'm not sure." I looked at Josie. Was it odd that Gina was asking about the victim of the fire? Would it have been one of my questions if my job had just gone up in smoke.

Attributing it to idle curiosity, she interjected before I could respond, saying, "Since it's not Louise, I was wondering if they know who the person was and could they have started the fire?"

"We have to wait for the police to make a statement."

"Yeah, makes sense. I gotta go. I'll text you when we're leaving."

Josie said, "Thanks, Gina. Please tell Louise we're thrilled to hear she's on the mend."

"Will do."

I placed my phone on the table and thought about Gina's statement. Did the victim really start the fire? "Josie, we witnessed arson *and* a murder."

5

I knocked on the front door at Louise's address, as listed on her job application. A dark gray sedan sat in the driveway, and I could see a cat snoozing on the windowsill, but no one answered the door.

Josie stood on the sidewalk. "Marty must be at work."

I knocked once more and waited, still nothing. "We can try later." I descended the steps and paused at the bottom. "This is a friendly neighborhood. The potted plants with deep purple and yellow flowers and the trailing ivy is stunning; the lawn is mowed, and even the side of the garage is neat with a tied recycling bag and a sealed box of Crossroad Brewery bottles ready for return. Does this place strike you as if an unhappy couple lives here?"

"Not really, but this is superficial. Marty may be particular about the exterior of the house, while Louise deals with the interior work, or vice versa. Many couples divide and conquer their household chores."

"Why do you think he wanted her out of the house?"

"I'm sure that's a question the police will ask both of them."

I glanced back at the house, fully aware of how deceptive appearances could be. "Do you remember the day of my party?"

Josie nodded. "I've been wondering the same thing. Louise and Marty appeared happy."

It was reassuring to know we were on the same wavelength. My cell phone pinged with a text: "It's Gina. They're back at her place, so we should get the car keys."

"Will you question Louise when we drop the car over?"

"Does my bread rise with yeast?"

She laughed. We walked the couple of blocks to Gina's place, and the door opened before I could knock. Gina gestured for us to come in.

"Hi. How's the patient?" I scanned the room, noting the stacks of newspapers on every surface and DIY books next to a floral recliner chair. She was so tidy at work that I wouldn't have guessed her living room would appear chaotic.

"Much better. Her vision has cleared up, she's hydrated, and she has eaten. There's one thing that's super important: the cooler in her car. When you get back, can you bring it in? It has her insulin and snacks."

"We can manage that. Is there anything else Josie and I can do?"

Her smile relaxed, a marked contrast to the last time we saw her. From my observations, Gina and Louise were close, but I wasn't sure why they downplayed their friendship.

"I have all we need, and I've made up the spare room for Louise. She'll stay here for a few nights and attempt to talk some sense into Marty. She's hopeful they can repair their relationship."

Josie asked, "Do you have any idea what they argued about that could have escalated to the point of her leaving?"

"Typical things, I suppose. Money, household chores, bad habits. You'd have to ask her to be sure. However, he was somewhat obsessed with tidiness and how he envisioned their place. Not the type of guy to leave a dirty spoon in the sink."

I nodded. "We stopped at their house on the way over and knocked, but no one was home."

"That's not surprising. He has a delivery route and works from sunrise until early evening. He takes care of vending machines at various businesses, refilling them as necessary. It's a good gig, and he also earns a decent commission. Louise mentioned that manufacturing plants are his best locations since the employees there can't leave to get drinks and snacks."

"That's interesting."

Gina extended a set of car keys and dropped them into my hand.

"Where should we park the car?"

"Next to mine in the driveway."

"Okay, we'll be back as soon as we can. We may need to take the long way since some firehoses could still be across the street. At least, there were when we walked over."

Her smile evaporated. "With everything that's happened, I forgot about the fire. I'm sorry for you and us."

"You can receive unemployment benefits while searching for a new job."

Her eyes widened, and her jaw dropped. "Are you ... firing us?"

I clasped her hand. "No. In reality, I have no idea when my bakery will reopen. It depends on so many factors that I can't control. The investigation into the fire, the death, my insurance company, a contractor—the list is endless."

"Right. The investigation. I think unemployment benefits will help in the immediate future."

"We're heading out. Do you need anything from the market on our way back?"

"No, I went shopping yesterday after work. My refrigerator and freezer are restocked. We can eat for weeks and never leave the house."

"All right then. We'll be back." I slipped the keys into my pocket. Josie and I strolled down the sidewalk, expecting to reach the car in about fifteen minutes or so.

"Gina's a good friend," Josie remarked.

"Do you find it strange that she asked if I was firing her and Louise?"

She said, "I'm sure that's because of the stress of the last eight hours and she's not thinking clearly. Louise and Marty had a blowout, which caused her to leave. She calls Gina, which is curious. Why didn't she stay with Gina for the night so she could talk to him when they were both calm?"

"Who argues with their partner and thinks clearly? Arguments lead to hurt feelings and words are said which can escalate emotions rapidly. We've all experienced this."

Josie fell silent. "If I had a fight with my boyfriend and needed a place to stay, I'd call you."

I shoulder-bumped her. "And I'd call you too. Just for the record, my guest room is always ready with fresh sheets and cozy blankets."

"Thanks; now all I need is a boyfriend to argue with so I can cry on your shoulder."

"How about you find a boyfriend and enjoy a wonderful relationship instead?"

She laughed. "I like your version much better than my doom and gloom."

"Check that out." I nodded toward the street. "The fire hoses are gone. That must mean the firefighters are confident that the blaze is extinguished."

"A ray of hope."

"Is that Officer Butler by Louise's car?"

Our pace quickened. "Hello," I called out.

She looked up; her face remained stone-like. "Ladies, I'm surprised to see you here."

"I thought you worked nights?"

"I do but there's something about this case that sunk its claws into me and I might as well work. What are you doing?"

"The hospital released Louise, and Gina asked us to take the car to her place. Louise needs her cooler with her insulin supplies. Is that okay, Officer?"

"It's Casey." Her brow furrowed. "I'm sorry, but you can't take the car. We need to process it for evidence. It's part of the overall crime scene, and since Louise doesn't recall what happened to her, we're hoping her vehicle will provide clues."

"Wasn't it a case of diabetic shock that led to her confusion, causing her to wander in the nature preserve and, fortunately, find her way to my house when the sun came up?"

Casey looked at me, her gaze steady. I replayed the last sentence in my mind. "How long does it take to slip into a diabetic coma?"

She said, "It depends on many factors, but it could be as quick as twenty minutes, depending on when she had her last dose and what she had eaten."

Josie said, "What are you thinking?"

"As a Type 1 diabetic, she knows how to manage her levels and stick to a schedule. If she had insulin, she must have also had a fast-acting form in case she needed it." I stepped closer to the car. "Is there any chance we could check the cooler?"

Casey unlocked the door. "Are you requesting to take essential medications to Louise Fletcher?"

"Yes?" The way she phrased her question must be following police protocol.

"As I thought. Before you proceed, I must examine and document the contents. The car will need to be brought in for processing. I should be able to release it in a day or two.

"Got it." I winked at Josie. "Picture time."

"For the record, I'm not listening to your conversation. I'm focused on the task at hand."

"Why, Officer Casey, did you just imply that my insight could be valuable to the case?"

She didn't look at me. Instead, wearing gloves, she pulled the small cooler from behind the passenger seat. Snapping open a large evidence bag, she placed the cooler inside and set it on the sidewalk. "Don't touch it. This is for precaution; I don't want anything inadvertently missed."

When she was busy documenting the contents, I said, "Your compassion for Louise is commendable."

She gave me a side glance. "Doing my job."

Josie peered through the car window. "If you were moving out of your home, you'd take all your belongings. But if you left in a huff thinking you'd be back in a day or so, you wouldn't take as much. Look at this. Louise packed three pairs of shoes and a duffel bag that must contain clothes. I've seen her wear a different outfit every day for three weeks. This looks more like a weekend bag, and since it's a VW, there isn't enough room for much more."

Leaning closer to the car, I took more pictures. I wasn't sure if Casey was listening to us so I dropped my voice. "Good point; we'll review these when we get back to my place."

Casey said, "I'm done. Just look with your eyes and give me your impression." After easing the top off, she put it behind the cooler. "What do you see?"

I reviewed the contents. "Ice packs, syringes, a bottle of insulin, and gel packs of glucose. Everything I expected."

She pressed her gloved finger on the ice packs. "Still solid."

"I guess this wasn't her first rodeo at keeping her supplies in a cooler."

"This is a high-quality freezer pack and should last several days if you keep the container mostly closed."

"She could have been on the road for a few days, then?" I raised an eyebrow. This was not something I expected; why wouldn't she always carry a glucose gel pack in her pocket?

"What else is in here?"

Was Casey challenging me? I reexamined the contents. "Snacks, juice, and water bottles. I pack snacks and drinks when I go out for the day. Am I missing something?"

"No. Just wondering." But she didn't elaborate any further.

Josie snickered. "You wouldn't want to see this one hangry."

"Are you diabetic?"

I replied, "No, I just become grumpy when I get hungry or thirsty."

She took photos with her cell phone, and I did the same when she wasn't watching. After closing the container, she looked at me and said, "I'll deliver this since I have several follow-up questions."

"Is there a chance we can tag along? I don't want Louise to think we didn't care enough to bring it to her."

Her brow arched. "I can't stop you from being in the same place as I am; please don't interrupt my questions or add any questions of your own."

"Even if they're beneficial to the case."

"Temperance, you are the key to this case. Whatever happened, it's connected to your bakery."

"Have you identified the victim?"

"We believe so."

"Have you seen the footage I sent to Sergeant Franklin earlier today? I included time stamps for important frames."

"The wrench you mentioned, we believe it was used to turn off the gas and it was found in the rubble. It has been sent for testing. If there are fingerprints, we will find them."

"It seemed that the perp was wearing gloves at the scene."

She nodded. "I noticed that too. Hopefully, when they picked it up from their workbench or purchased it, they weren't thinking about fingerprints. We might get lucky."

"You saw that they turned off the gas main."

She nodded. "Which tells me whoever did this wasn't looking for mass destruction. Are you sure no one has threatened you since you moved to town?"

Frowning, I said, "I've racked my brain, but it keeps coming up with nothing. And my email doesn't contain any clues, either. Someone used my bakery as a convenient location. There's one thing I wanted to tell you in person instead of putting it in the email."

"Oh? What?"

I had her undivided attention. "There are four master keys to my bakery. One is on my key ring, the second one Josie has, the third is in my home safe, and the fourth is on the key rack in my kitchen. The last time I remember seeing it was before I hosted a party at my place three weeks ago."

"Do your employees have keys as well?"

"Only to the front door."

"How many people attended your event?"

"Ten, including Josie and me." Withdrawing a piece of paper from my pocket, I handed it to her. "Here's the list—Gina, Louise and Marty, Alice and Peter, Erik Wool, and Celeste and Jonah."

She scanned the names. "Does anyone on this list stand out?"

I pressed my lips together and thought about everyone. "No, that's the issue. I consider everyone a friend, except I don't know Alice or Peter well, but we're friendly. He's my delivery guy."

She tucked the paper in her chest pocket. "Erik Wool was there. I will ask him if he heard or saw anything that, in hindsight, might provide insight."

Josie said, "Louise and Marty seemed to be in good spirits;

they were affectionate and appeared to be getting along. I considered them a very happy couple."

Giving me and Josie a contemplative look, she said, "Circumstances change."

I understood that what lay beneath the surface could often be deadly, and this case may have confirmed that.

"Casey, how can we help?" Josie asked.

"Stay out of the investigation," she said, giving me a pointed look. "You might find this difficult, given your tendency to analyze and find patterns. Maybe this time, there isn't one."

"There always are. It's unavoidable."

With a curt nod, Casey picked up the cooler. "I'm heading to Gina's now. You can ride in the cruiser or meet me there."

If we walked over, we would miss the questioning. "We'll take you up on the ride."

She smirked. "Have you ever been in the back of a police car before?"

I gave her a sweet smile. "Don't forget to let us out when we arrive."

With a laugh, she said, "I didn't want to like you, but you're growing on me. However, that doesn't mean I want you to interfere with my case."

I held up my hands. "We got it. No questions, only observations."

Josie asked, "Would you like us to share what we might observe after we leave?"

"Absolutely. Three sets of eyes are better than one." Casey opened the driver's door. "Don't forget to buckle up for safety."

I glanced at the VW. "What about Louise's car?"

"The tow truck is on its way." With a flicker of a small smile, she said, "I hope you didn't take too many pictures; that might be seen as interference."

With a laugh, I said, "Is there such a thing as too many?" We got in and closed the back doors.

Casey pulled away from the curb. She met my gaze in the rearview mirror. "Why did you quit your job?"

I looked out the window, not ready to share what had happened, not now, or perhaps ever. "I had an overwhelming desire to bake bread."

6

———————

*A*s the police car stopped next to the curb, Louise and Gina relaxed on the front porch in wicker chairs. Casey exited and opened the door for me, and I stepped out. Josie slid across the seat to join me.

I took the cooler from Casey's hand and climbed the porch steps. "Louise, here are your supplies."

Louise looked significantly better than she did this morning. "Temperance, I can't even tell you how much this means to me." A crease appeared in between her eyebrows as she scanned the street. "My car?"

I glanced at Casey, who remained silent. "Are you feeling better?"

"Much better, thank you."

Flashing a curious glance at Casey, Gina asked, "Will you join us?"

"Thank you." We sat down. "When we stopped at your house, I noticed the flowers were beautiful. Did you plant them?"

"Yes. I wanted pink and yellow this year, but Marty's color blind, and when he brought the purple petunias home, I thought, what the heck, the pink would be nice too. They've done beautifully out there."

Gina glanced between us and Casey, her lips slightly parted. "Not to sound rude, Officer, but is something wrong? I'm surprised to see you."

She inclined her head toward Louise. "I need to speak with Ms. Fletcher."

Louise clasped her hands in her lap. "You can ask me anything in front of my friends."

Until then, I hadn't realized she saw Josie and me as true friends. Given all she had endured, she must feel a strong connection with us, and collapsing in my front yard may have reinforced that.

Casey nodded. "Have you seen or spoken to Martin Thompson since you left home last night, after your argument?"

"No, he asked me to give him a few days to think about our future."

"Where did you go once you left the house?"

"For a while, I just drove around, and then I called Gina. I wasn't asking for a place to stay but letting her know she didn't need to pick me up tomorrow. My car was supposed to get an oil change tomorrow, but I called the garage and left a voicemail to cancel it."

"What garage?"

"Dooley's, just outside of town."

Casey asked, "What was your argument about?"

It was the same question Louise had sort of answered. I focused on her face to see how she'd expand on the details.

"The same old thing. Our future, I'm messy, I should find a better-paying job. You know, normal couple stuff." She gave me an apologetic look. "I told him I loved working at Early Rise and wasn't going to quit."

Her loyalty was appreciated, but a job in my small bakery

was nothing to quarrel about with her boyfriend. "I'm sorry he was unhappy with your job."

She waved a hand. "Don't worry about it again. He'll calm down once he has time to think about our silly argument. He always does."

With a sigh, she continued. "Every couple of months it's the same story, but it always blows over. I needed some space this time, so I packed some things. He needs to support my dreams, not torch them every chance he gets."

Gina asked, "Would you have gotten back together?"

"Yeah. I love the lunkhead. Besides, the bigger issue for us is my bad habit of picking up after myself. I tend to drop things and pick them up days later, that's just how I am."

Casey cleared her throat.

"If you don't believe me, just ask Marty. He'll be home from work around six."

"Ms. Fletcher, I regret to inform you Martin Thompson passed away last night. We discovered his body at the Early Rise Bakery."

I had never seen blood drain from a person's face before this moment. Louise's breath came in rapid, profound bursts. She pressed her fingertips to her temple and shook her head. "No. That's not possible. Marty's on his route, delivering soda and junk food. It's what he does every day." She squeezed her eyes shut, and a low wail emanated from deep within her. "No. No. No."

Gina rubbed her back. "Officer Butler, are you sure it was Marty?"

"Yes, his wallet survived the fire."

I asked, "How's that possible?"

Casey spoke in a formal tone. "At this time, I'm not free to discuss the details."

That I understood. "Did you find his vehicle?"

She nodded. "The truck was parked at the vending company's parking lot next to his usual van."

"How did he get inside the bakery?" Louise looked at me. "Temperance, I'm so sorry. He must have set the bakery on fire to force my hand to quit. I should never have left last night. We could have talked this out, and Marty would still be alive, and the bakery would be open for business."

That was a weak reason to burn down someone's bakery. However, I wasn't about to add to her distress. "It's not your fault, Louise. You weren't responsible for Marty's actions."

Gina asked, "Where do the police go from here? It's obvious Marty started the fire and died because of his actions. Is Louise financially responsible for the destruction?"

I said, "That's why I carry insurance."

Gina gave me a grateful nod.

"Louise, do you know anyone who might want to harm Marty? Did he have any co-workers who were angry with him? Perhaps someone competing for his route?"

Her voice was flat. "Not that I know of."

Josie leaned in closer. "Is there someone I can call for you? Marty's family?"

"No. That's something I need to do." Color began returning to her face. At least it wasn't as ghostly white as it had been moments ago.

"What led you into Green Stride Wood? Would you walk me through what happened?"

"May I please have a glass of water first?"

I stood. "I'll get it."

Gina nodded. "Thanks. The glasses are in the cabinet to the right of the sink."

Entering the house, I headed straight for the kitchen. Then, I turned around and went back to the porch. "Louise, would you like me to unload the cooler into the refrigerator?"

Her eyes focused on the floor, and her voice was soft. "I want to go home."

Casey said, "It's part of our crime scene. We are searching the house for evidence."

Slipping an arm around her shoulders, Gina said, "It's fine, Louise. You can stay here for as long as you'd like."

Louise lifted her eyes to mine. "Thank you, Temperance, that would be helpful."

I set it on the Formica table and opened the fridge. After sliding aside two bottles of Dashton pale ale, I placed the items from the cooler on the top shelf, allowing Gina to rearrange them later. Then, I put the cold packs in the freezer.

After filling a glass with water, I returned to the porch and handed it to Louise. The temptation to ask what I'd missed crossed my mind, but it would have been inappropriate. Josie could fill me in later.

"Let's talk about what happened after you parked your car near the bakery. Why did you go into the woods?"

She lifted a shoulder, her eyes still fixed on the floor. "It's quiet, and I needed time to think. I left my cell phone in the car to avoid Marty's apology call or, worse, to keep arguing. There's a bench near the pond where I sat for what felt like all night. I lost track of time and watched the sunrise. I didn't feel well, and since it was cold, the temperature fluctuations affected my insulin levels. Realizing I was in trouble, I discovered I didn't have any gel packs. I must have panicked and gotten confused. The last thing I remember was falling to the ground and picking myself up to keep going. The rest is hazy."

It had reached the low forties overnight. "That must have been just before she wandered into my yard."

"She was fortunate you were home," Josie said.

"Was it daylight at this point?" Casey quickly asked her question.

She nodded. I knew she had just mentioned the sunrise, but I understood Casey was gently poking for holes in the story.

"Did anyone see you?"

Her head snapped up. "You did when I was in Temperance's yard."

"Before that, say, between midnight and four o'clock?"

"No. I was alone. I left my house at nine, called Gina, and parked my car around eleven. I sat there for a while before taking a walk."

"No one saw you in your car?"

She turned slightly in her chair. "Gina, please let them know I called you."

"Better yet, I'll show you the recent calls on my phone. It's in the house. I'll be right back."

When Gina returned, she handed her phone to Casey. "Sorry, I had to find it. But you can scroll through the calls to see how long Louise and I talked last night. We spoke a couple of times."

Studying the phone, she looked up. "Gina, would you mind if I took a screenshot and sent it to myself?"

"Not at all. I'm here to support Louise."

I heard the screenshot snap three times and wished Casey would glance my way. I had questions. Instead, she returned the phone to Gina and thanked her.

"Louise, is there anything else you can think of that might help us determine how this tragedy happened?"

She slowly shook her head. "No. I'm at a loss for why Marty wanted to start the fire. He's always been such a kind-hearted man. We might have argued occasionally, but we always made up."

Gina bobbed her head. "I can confirm that. They fight. They make up. It's a pattern."

The pattern was complete.

Casey said, "Thank you for your time. If I have more questions, we'll talk again." There was no threat in Casey's words; it was merely a statement. However, Louise's eyes widened, and fear lingered within them.

Josie and I stood. "We'll give you some privacy. If you need anything, please call us."

Louise extended her arms, and I leaned down so she could hug me. Josie did likewise. "Thank you for bringing my cooler back. Officer Butler, when can I get the rest of my belongings and my car?"

"We need to review everything for evidence. I'll bring the car over as soon as it's released."

"All right, thank you!"

Josie went down the steps ahead of me, and when we reached the police car, I asked, "Casey, are you going to Marty and Louise's house?"

Giving me a side glance, she said, "Yes. Let me guess—you want to come along?"

I nodded. "Did you notice that Louise was upset but didn't cry when you told her Marty was dead?" I glanced over my shoulder. The two ladies huddled together, whispering. "And do you believe her story about sitting alone in the woods for hours without a better coat? And what happened to her shoe?"

"I'm not sure what to think. We witnessed her deteriorating condition at your place. She wasn't faking."

"Do you find it odd she would have left her car without medical supplies?"

Josie said, "It's possible she was distraught about the argument with Marty."

"If there's a pattern of Louise and Marty arguing about tidiness, I wonder how their place looks and if clues are hiding in plain sight."

Casey kicked the ground and looked around. "Against my better judgment, I'll allow you to come with me to that house. But again, observe with your eyes. If you notice anything, tell me."

"Why are you granting us access?"

"Sergeant Franklin believes this case revolves around

Louise. Although Marty may have started the fire, even with a second person appearing on camera, somehow, it's connected to her. After learning that Marty was the victim, the Sergeant acknowledges she's integral to the investigation beyond simply being lost in the woods." She opened the driver's door. "Like you, I'm suspicious and not above utilizing all my resources; you're an excellent asset. I researched you when I returned to the station."

Josie and I scrambled into the back of the cruiser before Casey could change her mind.

I didn't care why she agreed to our going, but lawful access to the house might have helped solidify the ideas that kept cropping up. "Have you found Marty's phone?"

She glanced in the mirror. "Not yet. I hope it's at the house. If I were going to break into a building and commit arson, I would have left it at home to avoid pinpointing my location. I think Marty took the key from your kitchen three weeks ago."

I watched as we drove past houses in Louise and Marty's neighborhood, eventually stopping in front of their home. "He must have been planning something for a while, just waiting for an argument."

Once more, the house struck me as tidy. What would the interior reveal? "Hold on a second. Why didn't Louise ask about her cat?"

"Stress?" Josie suggested.

The door was open, and the sergeant stood in the door-way. "Butler, I'm surprised you brought the ladies with you."

"You mentioned I should utilize my resources. Temperance is among the best in her field, so I'm engaging her as an unpaid consultant."

"Not anymore," I wanted to emphasize that I wasn't with the bureau any longer. "But I'm happy to consult."

His bulk filled the doorway. "It's like a fish out of water. A city girl from a big agency arrives in small-town USA."

"As a resident of this small town, I feel it is my civic duty to offer assistance if I can."

He stepped aside. "You know everything you see is confidential pertaining to an ongoing investigation."

Josie and I nodded, and I said, "Our lips are sealed." I felt compelled to mime a zipper motion across my lips to lighten the mood. Entering a dead man's home was sobering.

The inside was as tidy as the outside. I clasped my hands in front of me, and Josie did the same. I circled the living room. The kitty looked up from her sunny spot in the window and then closed her eyes again as if the presence of strangers tromping around her home was an everyday occurrence.

I stepped into a small dining area. Someone had tucked the chairs under the table, and a hutch showcased some collectible beer steins behind the glass. I proceeded into the kitchen, where a water cooler and a food dispenser for the cat clarified why Louise wasn't immediately concerned about it. "Casey. Officer Butler?"

Josie asked, "Did you find something?"

I pointed to the mugs in the sink and gestured toward the empty bottles on the sideboard. "It seems Marty had company last night."

Casey approached us from behind. "What did you find?"

"It seems that Marty and a friend enjoyed a beer last night, which contains a significant amount of carbohydrates that could impact a person's blood sugar."

"Are you suggesting Marty might have had company after Louise left?"

"She called Gina to vent. Who's to say Marty didn't reach out for a sympathetic ear, too? Also, you should double-check, but I don't believe that pale ale brand matches the bottles outside in the cardboard box."

She raised an eyebrow. "Not that this is much of a leap, but they're not?"

"No. Check the refrigerator."

Opening the refrigerator door, she peered inside. "I have a couple of bottles of Crossroad Brewery stout. Is that a different type of beer?"

I examined the bottles. "Yes. The person who came by to console Marty brought the beverages, and I served both types at my party. Now, I need to recall who was drinking which beer."

Josie asked, "Do you think that matters?"

Turning on my heel, I said, "It's all about the pattern."

7

———

*J*osie and I walked home from Louise and Marty Thompson's place, leaving Casey and the sergeant to gather any evidence. For me, the walk was about clearing away all unnecessary thoughts and concentrating on the extra beer mug and empty bottles.

"How can you be sure Louise didn't drink a beer with Marty before she left?"

"Think back to the party. He playfully teased her for only drinking light beer on rare occasions and for preferring red wine above all other adult beverages."

"Right," she said, nodding. "I remember that now. I found it insensitive of him to tease her in front of her friends."

"She would never drink craft beer. There was no wine-glass in sight. Whoever was with Marty had a beer, and did you notice the house was tidy?"

"I did. He must have cleaned it after Louise left which brings us back to your security footage."

"Let's assume Marty was the first person in the bakery. Why would he want to start a fire? Yes, he wanted Louise to stop working for me, but there are less dramatic ways to make her quit."

"Do you think he intended to burn it to the ground?"

We turned the corner at Mahogany Street; my house was near the intersection with Vine Street, where Josie lived. I walked in silence as I tried to reconcile the person I thought I knew with the man who set fire to my business. "He never showed any aggression toward me. I'll run a search to see if I can uncover any connection between Marty and other arson cases."

"Is that type of information easily accessible?"

"Most court records are available to the public. But they seal juvenile records. Unless he committed a crime before turning eighteen, I should be able to find the information through a basic search."

"Can I help?"

I gave her a broad smile. "I was counting on it. I'll take the desktop, and you can use the laptop. Working together will help us identify any patterns in his behavior that might explain last night's actions."

"What about the others at the picnic? If Marty didn't take the extra key, who else could have?"

"I've been thinking about the day of the picnic as well. Anyone who came in to use the restroom walked past the key rack, but it would have taken someone who knew the color of that key to guess what it could unlock."

"All the master keys are pink. Would Marty have known you used pink for the bakery."

"I don't see how he could. The front door keys are pale purple. I wanted to distinguish between someone's house and work keys. If Marty took the extra key, he would have looked for a purple key like Louise's."

"Who else besides you and me knew that the pink key was a master?"

"Gina and Louise would have seen my keys on the shelf at work."

Josie placed her hand over her heart, her eyes widening as she asked, "Do you think one of them took the key?"

With a heavy sigh, I cast her a sidelong glance. "It's quite possible. Louise could have, but why? Given her rocky relationship, was she planning to steal money from the cash register? At most, I leave a few hundred dollars in small bills and change in the register. I drop off a cash bag in the night deposit at the bank every day. There are no large sums of money on the premises."

"And Louise knows that, but maybe a few hundred dollars would be enough to get her on the road."

"Then why not ask for help?"

Josie linked her arm with mine as we trudged up my porch steps. "She had a case of tunnel vision. Was it possible she was trying to find a way out of an unpleasant situation? Maybe."

My shoulders slumped. "I need to speak with Louise and get some answers."

"She'll brush off your concern since it doesn't seem she lets people get too close."

"Except Gina." I opened the front door. Hank sat in the front hall, his little tail thumping on the rug.

I scooped him up. "Were you wondering when we would be back?" With a kiss on his head, I set him on the floor. "I'm going to my office. Are you coming?" He trotted ahead of us as if he understood every word.

"That pup is one smart boy."

I gestured to the chair across from my desk and unplugged my laptop, glad I remembered to charge it before we left. "Would you like coffee or water?"

With a laugh, she said, "Water, please. I'm down a quart."

I smiled. "Me too. Be right back."

As I walked into the kitchen, I stared at the key rack, wishing I could recall the events of the picnic. I hadn't been inside the entire time, and any guest could have taken the key without my knowledge.

I filled two glasses with water from the pitcher in the fridge and smacked my forehead. I rushed back to my desk. "I have an idea."

"Which is?"

"Did you take any photos on the day of my party?"

"No. I left my cell in my bag. Why?"

With a wink, I handed her a glass. "I took a lot of pictures at the picnic to post them of my first party on the bulletin board. You know, the team blowing off steam kind of thing. I saved them in a folder on my laptop, so I didn't think of them right away. This could clarify who was doing what and maybe even where." A tap on the keys displayed the images. "Take a look."

Josie came around the desk and leaned over my shoulder. Scrolling quickly through pictures of the food table and décor, I laughed, saying, "Pay no attention to these. I keep track of what I do at every party to avoid duplicating ideas."

"That keeps each party unique. I never thought to do that."

"All right. Here we go." I slowly advanced from one picture to the next. "Here's Gina with Louise and Marty. They're all smiles."

"A picture of people enjoying themselves."

In the next photo, Jonah and Celeste are talking with Peter and Alice. They looked close as he had his arm around her waist. "We'll need to talk with Celeste and Jonah. They could have overheard a conversation during the picnic or might have seen something this morning."

"You amaze me. How can you remain this calm? If my bakery were a pile of ash, I'd be curled up in a ball, crying."

"It wouldn't change anything. Finding information and patterns is doing something worthwhile. Even if Casey Butler or Sergeant Franklin don't use the information, they'll still have it, and it could lead to new clues."

"They're lucky to have you helping."

Without a doubt, Josie was in my corner. I sipped my water. "You know, it's interesting that Casey had a change of heart. Do you think it's because she knows I might uncover something?"

"That will make her impress her boss? Heck yeah, besides, she said that you were an excellent resource."

"You have a way of boosting my self-worth." I continued to examine each picture. Erik played bartender. "Look at this. He's handing my top suspects—Alice and Marty—bottles of pale ale, and Gina and Peter have one, too. It's not the same brand that was next to Marty's sink, but there's an important clue."

"And Louise appears to have a glass of club soda."

"Did you have any beer other than pale ale?"

"A stout, iced tea, lemonade, sodas, and several bottles of wine."

My finger hovered over the tab button. "Hello. Check this out—Alice is walking down the kitchen steps, and Louise is looking at her while Gina hovers in the background. Look at their faces: serious but not antagonistic."

"They save that for the day-old bakery items. Go to the next picture."

The following image was a picture of Hank basking in the sunshine. "That was the last photo I took at the party."

She frowned. "That's unfortunate. However, we've confirmed your guests know each other and were together in the same location at the same time when your key was likely taken."

"The answer to who and why are in these pictures. I can feel it deep in my bones." I scrolled back to the group scene where Erik was passing out beverages.

"It's unfortunate that the only picture I have of anyone

coming out of the house is of Alice." I enlarged that picture. "Does it look like she's holding something in her left hand?"

"Hard to tell. Can you print it so we can get a closer look?"

A few key taps later, the printer ejected the photo. Josie pulled it off, and I handed her a magnifying glass. "Do you see anything?"

Scanning the page, she handed it and the glass to me. "No." Her voice dripped with frustration.

"Reviewing details is a test of patience." I examined Alice's hands and the outlines of her jean skirt pockets, and I did the same with Louise's outfit and hands. There was nothing that resembled the shape or size of a key. I set it aside.

Scribbling the names of my suspects on a pad of paper, I tore the list in half and handed it to Josie. "Can you start with Alice Sullivan and Peter Swanson? Depending on what you find there and how far I've progressed with the other names, I might give you another one."

"Understood." She took a seat and the sound of keys tapping filled the silence.

"When you find information, copy the relevant section and paste it into a Word document."

"That's if I uncover something important."

"Be patient. Also, check social media accounts if their names don't appear in searches for arson or breaking and entering. We're not just seeking confirmation of criminal activity, but this can provide us with background information —friends, hobbies, and similar details. It helps build a character profile."

The grandfather clock in the front hall chimed the hour. Glancing at my watch, I stretched my arms overhead. "Holy cow! We've been at this for two hours."

Josie didn't look up. "I found out why Alice wants day-old items. I came across an old news story about her; she runs an after-school program where she teaches the children how to make nutritious meals and sends items home with anyone who wants them."

"Really?" I felt the deep furrows between my eyes. "Why didn't she ask for donations to the program? I would have set aside some items like I do for Mac's pigs."

"You should ask her that question. However, it's a great program based on my findings."

"Now I feel awful. In addition to losing my business, Alice also lost a food source for the kids."

"Peter Swanson has a solid reputation and bought the delivery business three years ago from his uncle. I can't find any negative information about him, and his social media features images of produce and little else."

"I researched Marty's background. It's clean and likely needs to be since he handles money and drives as part of his job. Traffic tickets could have been an issue if he were a speed demon."

"Is it possible that something he did as a kid was covered up?"

I leaned back in the chair. "That could apply to any of these people. Although I checked Gina and Louise's references when I hired them, today, I went a little deeper."

"What about Jonah and Celeste? Could they have been responsible for this?"

"They're not on my list of suspects. I can't imagine they'd want to burn it down after selling me the business. Besides, they're in their sixties. Those people in the video footage were smaller in stature and moved with ease. I considered asking Casey what the officers learned when they took statements from everyone at the scene, but her new cooperation will only extend so far."

"Well, I know nearly every shopkeeper in town and the clerks at the post office. I could ask around and see if anyone has been talking about the bakery."

I stifled a yawn. "That's perfect for tomorrow's task."

"I'm going to head home. Unless you'd like me to stay over?"

"Thanks, Josie, but that's unnecessary. Hank and I are going to have eggs for dinner, curl up on the sofa, and watch an old movie. Who knows, we might even conk out early."

I pushed away from the desk, and he jumped to his feet, tail wagging. "First, we'll walk you home and stretch his legs at the same time."

My pup danced around my legs. He knew that word and ran into the kitchen, then back to herd me in that direction so I'd put on his harness and leash.

"Who knows, maybe a fresh idea will spring to mind."

She placed the laptop on the corner of the desk. "Temperance, do you think someone targeted you, or was this a situation that spiraled out of control?"

"Definitely the latter. I don't think murder was on anyone's mind when they entered the bakery."

"Do you think person number two is feeling guilty now?"

"I'm certain. I need to believe it was an accident and they never intended to kill Marty. It still bugs me Louise didn't shed a tear."

"People process grief in different ways. Perhaps she's one of those people who can only cry alone in the shower or while driving."

"Possible, but not probable. She never flinched when Casey said he was dead; I watched her the entire time. Gina was more upset than Louise. Another thing we need to do tomorrow is talk to the ladies about the party, but I need to figure out how to broach the topic of the key to either get them to confess they took it or implicate who did."

"For the record, my money's on Marty. He knew Louise's bakery key was colored. It's not a stretch to believe that a different colored key could unlock the back door." Her face fell. "It's so hard to think someone we know killed a person and started a fire."

"People are often driven by reasons we can't understand when it comes to crimes of passion."

"Do you think that's what this was, a crime of passion?"

"Until I know for sure, I have to believe it was. I couldn't bear to think it was deliberate." I fastened Hank's harness and leash on and slipped on my sneakers. "Ready?"

Josie held the screen door while I locked the front door. The sky was showing colors of violet and magenta. Hank and I had enough time to walk Josie home and return before it got too dark.

We had gone a few hundred yards and were about to turn up Vine Street when Hank froze, growled, and the hair on his back bristled.

"What's wrong, baby?"

Jonah emerged from behind an overgrown yew bush in a neighbor's yard which led to the shortcut to town. "Temperance, there's something you need to know. It's about the key to your bakery."

One answer to a mystery. "What is it?"

He gurgled and pitched forward onto the sidewalk; a knife handle was protruding from his back.

8

————————

$\mathcal{I}$ dropped to my knees and pressed my fingertips to his carotid artery. The pulse was there but faint. "He's alive. Call 9-1-1!" I took my sweater off and pressed it around the knife, being careful not to dislodge it. If nothing else, I hoped to stop the blood flow spreading across the shirt. While I held his hand, I scanned the area but didn't see anyone nearby.

"Jonah, help is coming. Stay with me."

Josie provided details about our location and his condition. She said, "They're on their way."

His eyes fluttered as I gripped his hand more tightly. "Jonah, the ambulance will be here soon. Can you tell me who did this?"

"Key." The word was a whisper.

I glanced at her. "We can talk about the key when you feel better. Save your strength." If he survives, I didn't want to think that the arson case would claim another victim. Since he mentioned the key, these incidents must be linked.

He clung to my hand, as if our connection were tethering him to life. It was comforting to know he'd fight to live. The blood seepage slowed, which was a good sign, but I had no way of knowing the extent of the damage to his organs. If the blade had struck anything vital, he could be experiencing unchecked internal bleeding.

In the distance, the sound of emergency sirens grew louder. I handed Josie Hank's leash. "Can you hold him?"

She picked up the pup. "I'm going to wave down the ambulance. I'll be close by."

I scanned the area again but didn't see anyone. "Jonah, who hurt you?"

"I don't know." His eyes fluttered as if the effort to keep them open was hard.

Car doors slammed, and the sound of feet running on the pavement caused me to exhale. "Jonah, they're here. You're going to feel better very soon. Hang in there."

"Temperance."

Without looking up, I recognized her voice. "Casey, someone stabbed Jonah."

"The paramedics are right behind me."

Two women placed their gear on the ground. The brunette asked, "What can you tell us?"

"This is Jonah Young. Age approximately sixty. We were walking to Josie's when he stepped from the bushes. He said he needed to talk to me and then pitched forward. There's a knife protruding from his mid-back, and a lot of blood. I carefully tucked my sweater around the area to slow the flow."

"Did you try to remove the knife?"

"No."

"Please move back," the blonde requested.

"You're in good hands, Jonah," I eased my hand from his and walked over to Josie. Casey followed us.

Two more police cars arrived, and Casey provided the officers with a quick rundown before she turned to us. "Tell me exactly what he said before he collapsed."

I observed the emergency personnel taking his vital signs and asking questions as they examined the knife wound, leaving the sweater wrapped around it. If nothing else, it might have kept him from losing even more blood.

"Temperance? Today seems to be your day for people crumpling at your feet."

With a crooked smile, she tried to lessen the tension that was evident in my posture.

"Josie and I were walking to her place. Hank missed his walks today and needed to burn off some energy. As we approached the shortcut to South Street, behind the Wilks's house, Hank alerted us that something or someone was ahead. Jonah stepped out, saying I needed to know about the key, which I assume referred to my bakery. Before he could continue, he collapsed. Josie called for help, and I held his hand, encouraging him to hold on, hoping he'd say something more. But he only uttered the word, *key*, once more. The encouraging news; while I held his hand, his grip remained firm."

"That's good. Did you see anyone nearby before or after Jonah collapsed?"

I knew she was asking if I saw an assailant. "No, I scanned the area, and he said he didn't know who attacked him."

"In all likelihood, he doesn't know, but he may suspect someone. If you're unaware, stabbing in the back is an idiom for betrayal."

"It's one way to prevent someone from talking to the authorities. It's not like the victim can pull out the knife and apply a pressure bandage for themselves."

We watched the EMTs place Jonah face down on the gurney and strapped him in. She nodded. "I need to follow the ambulance. Are you going home?"

I shook my head. "We can hang around here while the team investigates."

"Stay out of it, Temperance. There's nothing you can do."

"We'll observe, nothing more."

"This person has just upped the ante. It's not safe."

I took Hank in my arms.

Josie said, "We'll go home."

I decided to give in. Casey was right, the attack on Jonah changed the game again. "That's where I'll be."

With a curt nod, she replied, "I'll let you know how he's doing. He should survive."

Jonah needed to—his attack added a complicated layer to this case.

Watching Casey stride across the street, I couldn't help but wonder if the officer ever slept. Since the fire, she had been on duty as long as I had been awake.

Josie nudged my arm. "Celeste."

The older woman zigzagged through the grass as she called for Jonah. Her eyes locked onto me. She changed direction, making a beeline for us. "Where's Jonah?" Her eyes were wide with fear, and her voice was shrill, teetering on the edge of hysteria.

"He's on his way to the hospital."

Her legs buckled, and Josie caught her before she fell to her knees. We helped her to the curb, each of us watching as the crime scene tape was unrolled and the area was sectioned off.

Her voice quivered as she asked, "What happened? He was supposed to meet me at The Sassy Slice for pizza. I ran to the post office, so he was going to get us a table. When I returned, no Jonah. I bumped into Alice Sullivan, and when she mentioned she saw Jonah walking down the street. It looked as if he was heading toward Mahogany Street.

I asked, "Why do you think he didn't stay at Sassy's?"

Her lower lip trembled as she shrugged. "I don't know. He didn't say a word to me."

"Did you see anyone else?" I locked eyes with Josie. "Other people dining?"

"No. Midweek, it's usually all takeout." She wiped her

cheeks with the back of her hand. "I need to get to the hospital."

"Please take a few more minutes to get your emotions under control. You won't be able to see him right away. The doctor will need to examine him, take X-rays, and perform other tests to determine the best course of treatment. For now, the best thing you can do for him is to take some deep breaths."

Josie said, "I'll drive you to the hospital whenever you're ready."

She shook her head. "No, Temperance is right. I need to steady my emotions and be strong for my sweetie." She squeezed our hands. "Can you sit with me for a few more minutes?"

"As long as you need." Hank rested his head on Celeste's shoulder.

We watched the police walk a grid pattern across the grass. "The Wilks's aren't home," I noted.

"Too bad. They could turn on their outside lights and help the officers as they canvass the area."

Celeste shuddered. "How did Jonah get here so fast?"

"The shortcut through the woods from South Street is one I take all the time when walking to the bakery." I had to remind myself—walked. Past tense. "It winds around the Wilks's side yard to the street."

"They don't mind people tromping through their property?"

Josie said, "It's been there for about fifty years. They were aware of it when they purchased the place."

"Oh, living on the opposite side of town, I never used it."

One officer set an orange plastic tent card on the ground and continued walking in a straight line. I wanted to ask what he had found, but remained seated on the curb. For now, at least, I was watching events as they unfolded.

Celeste gently rubbed Hank's ears. "I need to go."

I stood as Josie slipped her arm under Celeste's for extra support. She then hugged us, saying, "Thank you for staying with me."

"Please call us with an update whenever you have a moment. We hope he's going to be just fine," I nodded at Josie.

"I will." The hitch in Celeste's breath pierced my heart. I hated that she and Jonah were going through this, but I reminded myself it was about the fire, and how they were involved was a sobering question.

Her chin dipped. "I'll be forever grateful that you saved him." She walked to the corner of South Street, and then we lost sight of her.

I sank back onto the curb. "Who's going to be hurt next?"

Hank rested his head on my chest and nudged my chin with his wet nose. I loved how he tried to comfort me. "What if, when Jonah saw Alice while waiting for Celeste, he remembered something he had seen, that at the time seemed innocuous? Particularly Alice and Louise at the picnic after Alice came out of the house. She could have taken the key and given it to Louise, and Jonah could have witnessed it. At the time, it was nothing; however, since the fire, it dawned on him that he might have witnessed a theft."

"Running into Alice jogged his memory that people acted strange at the picnic?"

"Exactly. He was desperate to tell me."

"Alice followed and stabbed him before he got close enough for us to see her."

"The type of knife will be important in this case." I tapped my lips, closed my eyes, and pictured the knife. "The handle measured approximately three inches in length."

"Does it matter, and how do you know?"

"When I wrapped my sweater around it, I noticed where it met my hand. Most knives have a handle that is about five inches long. It's about balance; therefore, a shorter blade would require a shorter handle. Whoever did this grabbed a knife of convenience."

"So, it's not a pocket knife?"

I tilted my head. "It could be. There's no way to tell from a quick look at the handle, and I didn't notice a folding mechanism. I was afraid of it jostling and causing more damage. Casey will know for sure, and then it's a matter of checking for prints."

"As we get closer to identifying the players, more questions pop up. Is this typical for an investigation?"

Hank let out a sharp bark and wagged his tail. "Someone's getting anxious." I gazed at the scene before us. "Come on, I'll walk you the rest of the way to your place."

We ambled down the street with Hank's nose to the ground as I thought about Jonah. Our assessment had to be pretty close; I'd share my idea about Alice with Casey when she called—if she called later. Otherwise, I'd swing by the station tomorrow, check to see when the fire marshal would give his report, and bring her up to speed. We turned onto Vine Street, and Josie's house was midway.

"How about I drive you home? It's dark, and there's a killer on the loose."

A shiver raced over me. I didn't lean into fear, and if Jonah hadn't been attacked, I wouldn't have worried about walking Hank. "Thanks, Josie. A ride would be nice. Would you mind if I ordered a pizza for pickup on the way back to my place?"

Her eyebrows arched. "Are you curious about who might be hanging around downtown?"

I smirked. "Am I really that transparent?"

"Not at all but it's something I was thinking. And if you don't object, I could throw a few things in a bag and stay over. We could dissect the new clues over a slice or two."

Now I grinned. "A pizza with the works and a Greek salad."

Hank barked and pranced around our feet.

Josie laughed. "Someone thinks it's a fantastic idea."

I took out my cell and called in our order. "They said it would take twenty minutes for pickup."

"We can be there in five. It won't take long to toss some clothes in a bag. After that, we'll be in stakeout mode."

"Not that we might see anything, and if Casey knew what we were up to, I'm sure she'd discourage it."

"It's a good thing she's busy at the hospital." Josie unlocked her front door and switched on the overhead lights. "Give me two minutes."

"Take all the time you need."

She dashed down the hall, and Hank and I wandered into the living room. Standing in the semidarkness, I recalled the bakery footage and my suspects. Louise, Alice, and Gina were about the same height; Jonah was well over six feet, and Celeste stood just five feet tall, though I didn't consider them suspects. I closed my eyes, trying to remember Marty and Louise together as they stood with the others while Erik served drinks. My eyes widened. Except for Erik, the others shared a similar height. Marty and Peter were around five-eight. Any of them could have met Marty at the bakery. Gina had more curves, but both Louise and Alice were slender.

I've been focused on Louise being the one who followed Marty into the building, but what if the person who came out was the first person inside? Marty followed them. But why?

"Josie?"

"Coming." She walked down the hall with a tote bag slung over her shoulder and jingled the car keys. "Ready?"

I nodded. "During dinner, we need to review the picnic pictures again, and the footage of the break-in. I've just real-ized that we have multiple suspects. There are four possibili-ties of the person who left the bakery before it burned."

Her brow wrinkled. "How's that possible?"

"You'll see it when we look at the pictures. We might have been looking at this case through too narrow of a lens. Louise might not have left Marty behind. It could have been Alice or Gina."

"Wow. Did we go from a stakeout to new primary suspects?"

"Alice and Louise were together at the picnic. Louise and Gina are better friends than we realized. Jonah mentioned the key. Alice was at Sassy's and could have followed Jonah to the shortcut. She argued with Louise on the day of the argument with Marty and the fire. We need to dig deeper into Alice."

"Now, let's grab our pizza and dissect the details."

"But first, we'll check if anyone is lurking around. I want you to slowly drive down South Street. It's a perfect evening for a stroll, and we might get lucky."

Whoever was involved in the murder of Marty Thompson, would have made an obvious mistake. I aimed to discover what that mistake was.

9

———

$\mathcal{H}$ ank had his front paws on the passenger door, tail wagging, looking out the window as Josie crept down the street. I scanned the few groups of people on both sides of the street until we struck gold. "Up ahead. In front of Ruggles. Louise, Gina, Alice, and Peter are eating ice cream at a bistro table."

Josie let out a soft whistle. "Could they be in this together?"

"That's a lot of people who have to keep quiet. If I were planning a crime, the fewer people who knew, the better."

"You're a professional criminalist." She eased the car into a parking spot close enough to hear the foursome, yet still a short walk to Sassy's. I rolled down the window as she turned off the engine. I gently tapped Hank's nose, his signal to stay quiet. Since dachshunds are known for barking, I hoped he'd behave tonight.

Gina's voice was loud enough to hear her clearly. "Thanks for inviting us for ice cream. It's been a tough day for poor Louise. Getting out of the house and doing normal activities might help her sleep tonight."

Alice nodded. "Do you know why Marty was in the bakery?"

Louise shook her head and stirred her spoon in the paper cup, appearing indifferent to the sweet treat.

Josie pulled out her phone and tapped a note. *Can Louise eat ice cream?*

I shrugged and mouthed, *sugar-free?*

She nodded in agreement.

Louise cleared her throat. Her voice was strained. "It's hard to say what he was doing. After our argument, I never called to check in. I figured we'd make up today or maybe tomorrow, but I never expected that would be the last time I saw him." She sniffed and dropped her chin to her chest.

Gina slipped her arm around Louise's shoulders and said, "Of course you didn't."

Alice pursed her lips, and Peter shrugged. He remarked, "It must be tough."

"Still, don't you think it was weird for him to be at the bakery in the middle of the night?" Alice asked.

Louise shot her a sharp glance. "Are you trying to imply something?"

"There was a fire. Could your boyfriend have hated your job and Temperance Matthews so much that he'd want to burn the place down? I mean, that's one way to ensure you look for a new job."

"Alice," Peter said. "That's harsh."

"It's what everyone at this table is thinking. You heard him at Temperance's barbeque, and I quote, '*either quit your job or I'll help you quit.*'"

I took a deep breath and snuggled Hank close to my chest. What had I ever done to Marty?

Gina shook her head. "I don't believe that. He was all talk and no action."

"Until last night." Peter scraped the last of his ice cream

and tossed the cup into the trash bin. His eyes locked onto mine. He pushed back from the table and strutted to the car.

Josie saw him coming too and held out her phone. "This is what I was talking about. The hydrangea would look perfect in that spot in your side yard."

He leaned against the car door. As Hank grumbled, I said, "Easy, boy."

"Temperance, I wanted to say I was sorry when I heard about the fire. You were a good customer."

"Thank you, Peter, but I will rebuild and reopen. I am meeting with the police tomorrow to find out when they'll release the scene for cleanup."

He glanced over his shoulder at the ladies. "We were just discussing why Marty wanted to set fire to your place."

"Oh?" I hoped my voice sounded interested, not like we had deliberately parked here to eavesdrop on their conversation.

He nodded. "We've got no idea. Darn shame."

The timer on Josie's phone chimed. "Our pizza is ready."

"Dinner from Sassy's?" he asked, opening my door.

Holding Hank close, I got out. "I could use Josie's company tonight, and it's been quite the day. Besides, neither of us felt like cooking." I gestured toward their table, where the ladies didn't attempt to hide their interest in our conversation. "Just as Louise and Gina needed friends. It's been a tough day for a lot of us in town."

He stepped back. "Don't let me keep you. Soggy pizza is the worst."

I forced a smile. "Have a good night."

"You too."

We entered the restaurant. Josie paid for the pizza and salad while I hovered near the door. The restaurant didn't allow pets, but I didn't want to linger on the sidewalk either. Right now, I didn't feel like I could trust anyone in that foursome, well, maybe Gina. She'd known about Marty but stood by her friend.

I held the door open as Josie carried the box and bag. Peter stood near the car as if waiting for us. Did he think we were lying about getting a pizza?

I waved. "See you later."

He nodded. "Ladies."

Josie pulled from the curb and glanced in her rearview mirror. "He's still watching us."

I glanced in the passenger door mirror and guessed he'd stand there to make sure we had left. His behavior tonight surprised me. Until tonight I thought he was a good guy, now he projected an ominous vibe. Was there more to that conversation that would have been beneficial to hear?

"Do you think Casey Butler should be in the loop that Marty was browbeating Louise into quitting her job? It could be a motive."

"Louise mentioned it when we were at Gina's. I wonder if the medical examiner has determined how Marty died, smoke inhalation or another cause." I stared out the window, not registering the houses as we drove past. Hank was snoring softly on my lap. How a dog could fall asleep so quickly was beyond me.

After we arrived at my place, I placed the pup in his bed, found Casey's card, and dialed her number.

Two rings were followed by, "Butler."

"Casey, it's Temperance Matthews. Do you have a moment to talk?"

"Great minds think alike! I just turned down your street. Would it be all right if I stopped by?"

I crossed the room and turned on the porch light. "Sure. We have pizza if you're hungry."

"Thank you, but I'm fine. See you in a few." She clicked off.

"She's a friendly person, isn't she?" Josie grinned while setting plates on the table.

I prepared Hank's dinner and refilled his water bowl. "Efficient is the word that comes to mind. But she's warming up."

"That's because she knows it's smart to have you as an ally on this case, and keeping things friendly helps you funnel information to her."

"Be right back." The sound of a car door slamming drew me to the front hall. I stood on the threshold. Casey walked up the front steps, her face reflecting quiet sorrow.

"Do you have an update on the case?"

Scanning the area, she said, "We'll discuss it inside."

I had her walk in front of me as I surveyed the shadow-filled street. Nothing stirred. I closed the door. "We're just having dinner. Come on into the kitchen."

"Is someone with you?"

"Josie. After the Jonah incident, we decided to stay together tonight."

With a brisk nod, she replied, "Probably for the best."

I pulled out a chair. "Have a seat. Would you like coffee or water?"

"Coffee if it's brewed."

I turned on the Keurig and placed the cup under the spigot. "Decaf or regular?"

"A dark roast if you have it. I'll be relying on caffeine for the foreseeable future."

Josie asked, "How's Jonah?"

"He's a lucky guy and will be fine. The knife was a little over two inches and missed any vital organs. Either the perp didn't know where the best place was to stab him for maximum damage or didn't intend to kill him."

I handed her the mug of coffee. "Have you questioned him?"

"Not yet. He's in recovery and won't be awake for a few

hours. After he is, I'll interview him and see what I can learn."

"That's excellent news." I pulled out a chair and sat down, taking the plate Josie handed me with an oversized slice of pizza. "If you change your mind, feel free to help yourself. We have plenty."

Casey smiled. "Thanks. I wanted to let you know the preliminary report on Martin Thompson has come back."

Pizza forgotten I focused my attention on Casey. "By the look on your face, he didn't die in the fire."

"No. A lethal blow to the head."

"Was it instant?"

"Yes." Her gaze remained steady. "At least he didn't suffer."

I understood what she said. "Whoever left him in the building was trying to cover up the murder."

"It may have been involuntary manslaughter, but we won't know until the investigation is complete."

Josie asked, "So if the person who left Marty in the building is discovered, can you find out what happened?"

"Not if—when. And yes, we know the accelerants were all items from inside the bakery—bags, boxes, cardboard, and powdered baking supplies. The ignition source was a lighter found near the victim."

My heart sank as I pushed back my chair and circled the table, my mind racing. "He died before the fire started, so did the second perpetrator add oil to make it burn hotter and faster?"

Casey continued, "That's my take. I'm not sure if you're aware, but coconut and olive oil burn at 350 degrees, while vegetable oil ignites at approximately 450 degrees. Given that the burning temperature of butter is 250 degrees and it was kept in the refrigerator, it couldn't have contributed to the fire. What do you use in your baked goods?"

"All of the above. Were there empty containers near the blaze or just at the point of origin?"

Her face was grim. "The fire investigator found remnants of metal oil containers on the floor, close to the refrigerators and not in the center of the room, where the fire started."

Josie said, "I know nothing about fires, but could tossing the containers aside have been an afterthought? Like someone changed their mind and wanted to keep them out of the fire?"

I said, "Remember, at three fifteen, we saw a light in the storage room that's where the oils are kept. Perp two shut the door and tossed the wrench fifteen minutes later." I sat down. "Follow my train of thought for a moment. Person one enters and prepares the area where he plans to start the fire with paper goods. In his mind, it could be seen as minor vandalism. Let's assume that was Marty. Tonight we overheard Louise, Gina, Alice, and Peter saying Marty mentioned if Louise didn't quit her job, he'd help her. Burning the bakery would have put her out of a job.

"That makes sense. Continue, but I have questions about how you overheard that conversation. We'll circle back."

"Marty turns off the gas main and enters the bakery using the key he took from my place. Jonah tried to give us information about the key and got stabbed for his effort. He ransacks the place and creates a small area to start a fire. Person two arrives, they argue and the newcomer hits him on the head with the wrench. He's dead. To cover up the murder, the perp starts the fire. But before they do, they add oils to make the flames burn faster and hotter."

Josie put her dinner aside, intent on my theory. "Who would know what products in a bakery would be flammable?"

"People who work in a kitchen should." My voice sounded hollow in my ears. "This brings us back to Louise. We know she argued with Marty earlier and by her own admission has no alibi for the time of the fire."

"And her car was discovered on the street," Casey said.

"But she wasn't wearing the same clothes as the person in the footage." Josie shrugged. "How is that possible? Oh, wait, could she have ditched them in the woods?"

Over my shoulder, Casey stared out the window.

Placing my hands flat on the table, I leaned forward. "You found a hoodie. Was it near the pond?"

She never flinched. "You shouldn't have left your job. You're quick."

"It's only logical based on your lack of a reaction."

She raised an eyebrow. "I thought you weren't a profiler?"

"We still had to complete the required coursework. If you found the sweatshirt, can you connect it to Louise?"

"Not yet. We didn't discover any hairs or other fibers that could help, but that doesn't mean we won't."

"It could have been out there for a few days." I leaned against the back of the chair.

"Doubtful. We had heavy rain the night before. Had this been dropped before last night, it would be soaked or at least muddy from lying on the ground. But it wasn't."

"Huh." I looked at her. "I'll bring you up to speed on what we've discovered since you left. Celeste had been looking for Jonah, who was supposed to meet her at Sassy's for dinner and found us. According to her, Alice saw him walking toward the shortcut. After we told her what had happened, she rushed to the hospital. But that got us wondering if anyone else was hanging out in town. Hence our pizza, and we left early to take in the sights."

Casey snorted. "Like you weren't trolling for clues? Right."

"We know that." I gestured in a circle around the table. "But to anyone else observing, it would seem we were downtown picking up a pizza after a long, emotionally charged day."

"Was that when you saw your suspects?"

"Yes, when we learned about Marty's threat to Louise—it wouldn't be the first time a couple's argument went too far. Unfortunately, Peter noticed us sitting in Josie's car and came over."

Casey shifted in her chair. "That could have been dangerous."

Josie said, "You should have seen Temperance diffuse the situation; it helped that we had ordered dinner."

"What can I say? It's always good to have kernels of truth on your side in every situation. We had a perfectly believable reason for sitting in the car," I smiled at Josie. "And this one had a timer that went off when it was time to pick up the pizza."

"Wow. Color me impressed." She offered us an appreciative smile. "Not that I condone your investigation of the crime. But I'm glad you're on the right side of the law."

"The next step is to convince Louise to confess." I picked up my slice and took a bite. "A thought occurred to me. We're assuming that Jonah talked to Alice. But in the pictures from my party, they never interacted. So, would Alice have spoken up to help Celeste find her husband?"

Josie asked, "Why not? It's not as if we're all strangers. They were at your party."

Casey said, "I see where your thought process is going. Until Jonah wakes up, we can't know for sure who he talked to and what he had to tell you."

"To be transparent, I asked Celeste to call me when he's ready for a visitor." I wanted to know what was so important that he had to see me. "He said, '*It's about the key to your bakery.*' Does that mean he had the key, knew who took it, and why did he think it was relevant to discuss with me?"

"I understand you're eager to speak with him. I would appreciate it if you would let me talk to him first."

"Can I be in the room when you do?"

She shook her head. "You can't. It's official police business, and you're a civilian, even though you are an asset to this investigation. I've already bent many rules to allow you in this far."

She was right, but if he had known who had taken the key, it could have led to person two from the bakery. "Casey, did you give Jonah a protection detail?"

asey sipped her coffee. "Temperance, that's been taken care of. Jonah is safe."

I exhaled, giving her a faint smile, and said, "I knew you would, but it made me feel better to say it out loud."

"I understand. This is connected to the fire, and you bear the burden, but you shouldn't. You didn't start the fire or even provoke it. The responsibility lies with those trying to cover up the death of Marty Thompson and starting it. Even if he did, someone attacked him, and we don't know if they realized he was dead or too heavy to drag out of the building. Either way, they walked away from a burning building, and that's criminal."

Josie said, "I hate to think that someone we know is responsible for any of this. I read about this kind of stuff in the newspaper or watch it on the nightly news, but it doesn't happen in Oak Hollow."

With her coffee cup empty, Casey stood. "I need to get back on patrol, but if you need me, just call, or if any new ideas come up, text."

"Aren't you exhausted? You were awake all night and

most of today, and you're still protecting the community. That's a lot for one person."

"I'm not a great sleeper and don't have a family, so work keeps me busy."

What about friends, lingered on my lips, but I didn't ask. Casey Butler was a newcomer like me; perhaps she hadn't made friends. I wouldn't know many people if it weren't for Josie and my customers. Casey worked the night shift, and it was a solitary life.

I walked her to the door. "Thanks for the update. I understand sharing information with me in these circumstances isn't typical, but I assure you I will keep everything confidential."

She gave a quick nod. "The chief and sergeant believed you'd be an asset and gave the green light to keep you informed."

I waited until she was inside her cruiser before closing the door and turning off the outside light. Hank stood in the archway to the kitchen, tilting his head to the side. "It's been quite a day."

Woof. He wagged his tail and trotted over to his bed. Josie had poured two glasses of red wine.

"I thought we could benefit from a bit of relaxation."

"It's been a day." I lifted my glass and clinked it against hers. "Here's to a better tomorrow."

THE SKY WAS OVERCAST, and dark clouds hung heavy with the promise of rain when I looked out the kitchen window. I loved rainy days because they brought customers into the bakery for a cup of coffee and something delicious, and bread sales soared as people enjoyed soup and chili for dinner.

Today, my mood mirrored those clouds. Instead of rain, I held back tears I couldn't shed yesterday. Josie padded barefoot into the kitchen and went straight for the coffee pot. She wasn't a morning person.

"How long have you been awake?" She handed me a mug.

"Since four, my internal alarm went off as if it were an ordinary day."

She propped her head on her hand and sipped the coffee. "Did you grind the beans?"

"Yeah, I had nothing better to do." A tear slid down my cheek. "When I woke up, I thought I had a nightmare. One person is dead, another is in the hospital, and my business is gone."

"I've been thinking about everything, and even if you believe it's too soon, please hear me out and give it consideration before you say no. What if you started a micro bakery? Get your kitchen certified for home baking. You could begin with loaves of bread. If that goes well, you might expand into cookies and muffins. I was scrolling online before falling asleep last night, and it's a trending concept across the country."

"I don't have a storefront to sell baked goods."

"But you don't need one. That's the beauty of this idea. We can find a handy person to build a small stand. Heck, I even saw a micro bakery using an old reclaimed armoire, or was it a small greenhouse? You'll need to check with town hall about the requirements for putting something in your front yard, like near the sidewalk, but this is doable. I'll help you get everything set up. It will be Early Rise 2.0."

I shifted in my chair. *Was it too good to be true?*

She hurried into the living room, returning with her laptop. "Just take a look at what I found and think it over. While your store is being rebuilt, you can keep your customers engaged. Even for the holidays, you could offer specialty breads. All of this would be on a smaller scale than you had before, but it's a step forward."

I scrolled through the pictures on social media that Josie had ready. "They're cute, but do you think the town will go for something like this?"

"Why wouldn't they? Besides a home inspection, during which you might need to make minor modifications, such as installing a professional dishwasher, you already have a commercial range with double ovens and refrigerator. You'll need to create an equipment list, and I'll go with you to the restaurant supply store. It'll be fun. I can assist with baking too, until you get up and running. "

Her enthusiasm was infectious. "The brick-and-mortar bakery won't be ready for months; this would stop my customers from finding an alternative source for some items." A flicker of hope sparked. "It's like people who put coolers out to sell eggs."

With a laugh, she said, "That's the basic idea, but you'll need to do the work. With eggs, the chickens take care of production. "

"Did you look up the town bylaws?"

Her eyes twinkled. "Can you bake bread?"

Josie's ideas pushed aside the clouds hovering in my heart. "Show me."

After a few taps, she turned the laptop around and sat next to me. "Shazam! The office hours are listed. You're in luck; the inspector's in the office this morning."

"At least one thing seems to be going in my favor," I said as I scanned the requirements. "For a cottage kitchen permit, I'll have to move Hank's bed and other items. He can't have access to the kitchen. Oh, wait, it needs to be separate from my personal kitchen." The clouds slid back in, and I pushed the laptop aside. "That was a great option while it lasted."

Josie jumped to her feet, hands on her hips. "Temperance Matthews, are you really giving up after reading for less than ten minutes? What would your Aunt Penny say if she heard you?"

My eyes widened in surprise at her tone. "Yes, I have a great kitchen, but the rules state…"

She raised her hand like a crossing guard displaying a stop sign. "And you own a large Victorian home with a housekeeper's efficiency apartment. Why can't you turn that into your cottage kitchen?"

"That was in case I needed to rent the space for extra income."

Her brows arched so high I thought they'd hit her hairline. "Your business burned to the ground, and until that mess is resolved, you don't have an income and plenty of time on your hands." She thrust her fist in the air. "Carpe Diem." With a glance my way, she asked, "Are you going to leave me standing in your kitchen with my arm in the air?"

Laughing, I said, "You've convinced me it's worth looking into. But first, how about a walk-through of the apartment to see if this idea is feasible?"

Beaming, she said, "Give me a couple of minutes to get dressed, and I'm your PIC."

I narrowed my eyes. "What's that?"

"Partner in crime. Or in this case, your baking business, except we're not partners. I'm just your bestie, pushing you out of the doldrums you're sinking into. Not that I'm suggesting you don't have a right to be down."

I pulled her into a hug. "I don't know how I was lucky enough to meet you the first time I visited my aunt, but that day was the luckiest of my life."

"Mine too." She hugged me back. "Be right back."

I said, "Me too."

Hank let out a joyful bark, wagging his tail. We reached a consensus. The day was getting brighter.

Entering the small apartment adjacent to the kitchen felt like stepping back in time. While my kitchen embraced the twenty-first century, the tiny galley kitchen remained firmly rooted in the sixties. I made a slow circle. "If I were to utilize this space, I'd need to gut the kitchen and living areas to create a commercial kitchen, but there's ample square footage. I'd keep the bedroom as my office, and a bathroom is always essential. The white tile work and fixtures are in pristine condition." Back in the main area, I closed my eyes to visualize how the space could look with the furniture removed, commercial-grade appliances added, shelving along the walls, and a central island for an abundant workspace. "This will be a significant undertaking, along with creating a space in the front yard."

"It could work, right?"

The smile on Josie's face would brighten even the darkest day. "I'll need to get estimates and talk to the building inspector to obtain a copy of the rules, but it just might. That's if your offer of help still stands."

She slapped me a high five. "I knew it. The potential's unlimited, and who knows, maybe you'll decide to keep your bakery micro-sized and give up the one in town."

Laughing, I shook my head. "Let's not get carried away. I love owning the bakery."

"True, but owning this could give you more free time. Who knows, you might be able to open stands all over the county."

"Hey, what about the free time you were just talking about? In one breath, I get a lighter load, and the next, you're adding to my baking schedule."

She looped her arm through mine. "Isn't it nice to have options?"

I squeezed her arm. "Thank you for reigniting my dream."

"You would have done the same for me. Now, I'm going to make a few calls to see if we can find someone to do the work. But first, we'll need to get this furniture out. Maybe you can decide which pieces you want to keep and what you could donate to charity. Next on the to-do list will be visiting town hall to apply for a permit."

"I'll walk Hank, and we can zip into town."

"Not so fast. We won't get far on empty stomachs, no matter how much pizza we ate last night."

"All right, first breakfast, a quick Hank stroll to the pond, and then town hall."

My cell phone rang, and I took it out of my pocket. "It's Celeste," I said, "Hi! How's Jonah? Oh, hold on." I pressed a button. "Okay, I have you on speaker so Josie can hear."

"Hi dolls, I have the best news ever. Jonah came out of surgery and the recovery room around eleven last night. I spoke with the doctor who operated, and he said my sweetie was one lucky guy. Zero damage from the blade, and after he rests and receives a pint or two of blood, he should be discharged in a day or so. "

"That is wonderful news, Celeste."

Josie said, "You must be so relieved."

"We both are. That's one reason I'm calling, but the other is that Jonah insists on speaking with you today. Visiting hours start at noon, so could you be here then?"

"You can count on us," I said. "Has Officer Butler come by yet?"

"She was here bright and early. I waited outside while they talked because it was official business. But did you hear that he has a guard at his door?" She sniffed, and I sensed the toll Jonah's attack had taken on her. "Is he in some kind of trouble?"

"Oh Celeste, did you ask Officer Butler about it?"

"No. As soon as she finished talking with him, she strode out of the room as if she had hornets in her hat. Her face was so tight, and her mouth could have been a ruler; I've never seen anything like it.

That was quite the image Celeste painted for us. "She takes her job very seriously."

"That was clear as a pane of glass. Can I tell Jonah you'll be here at noon?"

"We'll be there. Would you like me to grab you some lunch or coffee?"

"No, I'll get something from the cafeteria. However, I appreciate the offer."

Josie said, "If you think of anything, just call, and we'll bring it with us."

"Thanks, dolls. I'll see you in a couple of hours. Bye."

"Bye." The moment the line disconnected, I called Casey. "I want to find out what she'd discovered since Celeste's description of her demeanor was curious."

The call went straight to voicemail. After leaving a message requesting a return call, I frowned and slipped the phone back into my pocket.

"What are you thinking?"

"Jonah told Casey what he's going to tell us. But I want to compare notes."

She nodded. "What if he lied to the cops and would share the real details only with you?"

"Us. I'm not going there without you. We're in this hunt for clues together."

A sharp rap on the front door set Hank racing from the apartment, barking his special alert at me.

Following him, I closed the apartment door and hurried to answer it. Through the glass, I saw Casey's back. "Hey, I just tried to call you."

She nodded. "Can I come in?"

I opened it wider, and she stepped inside. "Hi, Josie."

"Would you like a coffee?"

She shook her head. "No thanks. I'm just coming off duty and heading home to sleep for a few hours, but I wanted to keep you in the loop. I figured by now Celeste called you. Jonah wants to be the one to tell you."

"You've got our attention. Tell me what?"

"Jonah believes it was Peter who stabbed him."

"Why? He hasn't even registered on our radar as a

suspect, apart from being a little creepy last night while approaching the car. What do you think?"

"Did you know that Peter and Louise dated years before she started going out with Marty?"

Josie's mouth dropped open. "Now, that is fascinating news."

"Are you thinking he had a beer with Marty, got him riled up, and convinced him to vandalize the bakery?"

Josie glanced from Casey to me. "What's the motive? Could he still have feelings for Louise and hope to break them up while egging Marty on about the job?"

Casey said, "What do you think?"

"It's a stretch," I pressed my lips together. "What if Peter had gotten under Marty's skin about Louise quitting, and Marty went to the bakery to vandalize it, and somehow things got out of hand? But if that happened, who was person number two? Louise or Peter?"

11

————

*A*fter Casey left, more questions swirled in my mind about the case, but I needed to refocus on my future. Later, while taking several pictures of the apartment and creating a rough sketch, Josie and I walked into the town hall.

The marble floors and spacious hallway was churchlike. Multiple closed doors led to various departments. I checked the directory to confirm the location of the building inspector. I whispered, "I can't believe I'm about to pivot again."

"It might be scary, but I promise it'll be good." She yanked open the wood door. She grunted. "It's heavy."

Pulling with her, I was surprised at its weight. What kind of office were we walking into? Were building records that precious?

A young man stood behind a waist-high counter. "Good morning. How can I assist you?"

With a confidence I wasn't certain I felt, I said, "Yes. I'd like to speak with Elaine Snyder about the guidelines for a cottage kitchen."

"Are you the woman whose bakery just caught on fire?"

Nodding, I managed a smile again. "Yes, that's me. I'm working on a plan to reopen."

"That's great! You make the best banana chocolate chip muffins I've ever had." He looked around, even though it was just us. "Just don't tell my mom."

I placed a finger to my lips. "Your secret is safe with me."

"Anyway, Ms. Snyder will be back in a few minutes. I can print off the application and a copy of the rules for you to look over while you wait."

"Thank you; that would be helpful."

He tapped the countertop. "I'll be back in a jiff."

Josie's eyes sparkled, and she winked. After the young man disappeared into a back room, she said, "Best banana muffins in town. That's high praise."

"I suppose I'll need to keep them on the menu or, even better, drop off a half dozen once the new kitchen is operational."

He hustled to the counter, holding a folder in his hands. "Here you go, and if you need anything else, just ask for me. I'm Jonathan."

I held up the folder. "Thank you. Should we sit over there?" I gestured toward a row of four chairs against the opposite wall.

"Yup. This way, you won't miss Ms. Snyder when she returns."

I handed Josie the rules and took the application. After scanning it, I said, "Add to the list, I'll need a building permit for the renovation. There's a section on the form which asks for the name and business license number of the company or person."

"Dotting the i's."

With an internal sigh, I scanned the rest of the application. This was going to be a bigger undertaking than simply placing a table on the front lawn with baked goods for sale. Was I ready for the challenge?

A woman walked through the door carrying a pair of work boots and a hard hat. She was dressed in jeans, a long-sleeve blouse, and brown penny loafers.

"Hey, Jonathan. Anything happening?"

He pointed at us. "The ladies have been here for a few minutes."

She smiled as she looked over. "Hi, how can I help you?"

We stood, and I extended my hand to shake hers. "I'm Temperance Matthews. I'd like to discuss the requirements for a cottage kitchen at my home."

"Come into my office so we can talk."

She rounded the counter, and Josie and I followed her into an office. "Please take a seat."

"Thanks."

"So," she said, placing her boots by an empty umbrella stand and glancing between me and Josie. "You want to open a small business?"

"I do. Josie is here as my coordinator."

"I see."

It didn't matter whether she understood Josie's role; all I needed to know was how complicated and expensive this new venture would be. "There was a fire in my bakery early yesterday morning, and I estimate it will take about fifteen to eighteen months before I can reopen." I extended the time to rebuild since I had no idea how long it would take, but doubling my original estimate wouldn't hurt.

"Was that your bakery? I'm truly sorry. It's tragic that the arsonist lost his life in the fire."

Nodding, I said, "It was awful, but I don't want to remain idle for as long as it takes to reopen. Josie suggested the idea of a micro-bakery and selling products from a small structure in my front yard. If possible, I'd like to keep some of my customer base so they won't have forgotten about me by the time I can return to full production."

She smiled. "As a loyal Early Rise Bakery customer, I

assure you that no one could ever forget the magic in your baked goods. I'm a huge fan of your sourdough cinnamon roll."

"Thank you! That's great to hear. I'll add that to my baking list."

With a laugh, she said, "You'll need to text me. It's a quick seller. I discovered the key was to arrive right after you open on Saturday, or else they'll be sold out."

Opening her laptop, she glanced at me. "Have you gone over the guidelines for the permit?"

"Yes, I have a small apartment attached to my home. I can convert the dining area and kitchen into a bakery while keeping the bedroom as my office and storage room. Of course, the bathroom will stay as it is."

"Have you started construction yet?"

With a glance at Josie, I said, "No. I'm meeting with contractors for estimates, but I wanted to make sure I was on the right path before wasting time or money."

"Smart move. How about I come by your place this afternoon? We can walk through the space. I can give you my thoughts on following the guidelines. Also, if you need names of contractors, I might know of others you can contact in case everyone is busy."

"That sounds great! Are you sure you have time?"

"I can be there at one."

"Oh, I'm not sure if I'll be back. We're heading to the hospital to visit a friend who was injured last night."

Elaine shut her laptop and placed her hands on the desk. "Jonah?"

How had she heard about that? "Yes. We found him, and Celeste called to ask if we could stop by to see for ourselves that he's doing much better." It was a slight stretch of the truth, but I wasn't going to share any details that could be misconstrued and used as fuel for the town's grapevine.

"I heard there was a lot of blood." She visibly paled. "I'm

friends with the Wilks, and when they got home, they said the police were still there searching for evidence. Is the assailant still at large?"

"Authorities have yet to release any information to the public, so I'm unclear about the investigation's status."

Josie's brow twitched. Was she surprised by the formality of my response? Old habits surfaced in from time to time.

"It's no longer safe in our small town."

"Don't worry. The police are doing an excellent job, and I'm confident they'll arrest the culprit."

She licked her lips. "When I saw Gina and Louise last night, they mentioned Marty wasn't a nice guy, and got what he deserved."

That was a cold statement. No one deserved to lose their life at the hands of another. But that wasn't something I'd discuss with Elaine. "You're friends with the ladies? They work for me. Well, did."

"Yes, we got friendly when I became a regular at the bakery. We meet monthly at various restaurants for cocktails and nibbles. Last night, we met for a pint at Bistro 9. It was good for Louise to take her mind off things. The topic of recent events was off-limits. Instead, we focused on the new craft beer from Dashton Brewery, a pale ale we'd been wanting to try."

This was my chance to see if the beer mug we found in the sink might have belonged to Louise. "I didn't think Louise drank beer."

"She enjoys a pint now and then. She has to eat, or it can wreak havoc on her system. We always make sure to order appetizers, and we never drink dark beers. I prefer to see through them."

"What did you sample last night?"

She gave me a sharp look.

Smiling politely, I said, "I haven't had the chance to dine

at the bistro yet, and I thought that if you could recommend something, it might entice me to go."

Her face softened into a smile. "The menu is amazing. I've never made a bad choice, and there isn't anything I wouldn't recommend, but they're heavy on the spice. They have an extensive selection of beer and wine if that's your drink of choice."

Josie had remained silent during the conversation and said, "We should make a point to go in the next few nights."

I knew what she was thinking. Maybe we'd run into Gina and Louise again.

"You won't regret it. Now, let's get back to me stopping by."

I wrote my address on a slip of paper and gave it to Elaine. "If that works with your schedule, I'll be home by two."

"I'll make certain it does," she said, standing as she shook my hand. "I'm sorry for the circumstances that brought you here, but it was a pleasure meeting you. I look forward to the opening of your little bakery."

"And I'll tell you the first time I bake those sourdough cinnamon rolls."

"Please let Jonah know I said hello and hope he recovers quickly."

"Thank you, Elaine, and we'll see you later."

Once we got outside, I stretched my arms over my head to loosen my shoulders and back. "That was more stressful than I had expected."

My eyes were drawn to the remains of my bakery. The blackened appliances jutted from the ash and rubble. "I'll hire Russ to get this mess cleaned up as soon as possible."

"That's a great idea. He may have a suggestion for the new project as well."

Propping my bag on my bent knee, I rummaged and found his business card. "I'm calling him right now."

"I'm going to grab us a coffee from Bistro 9."

"Are they open this early?" That was a weird thought. I had no idea what other businesses did during the day.

Josie walked backward, laughing. "Of course. There's an entire world in operation while you're baking. But for the record, their coffee isn't as good as yours."

I was about to dial when I asked, "Can you find out what kinds of beers they carry from Crossroads and Dashton Breweries?"

"Consider it done." She jogged across the street while I dialed Russ.

A deep male voice said, "RP Contracting."

"Russ? It's Temperance. Hello."

"Hi. I didn't expect to hear from you today. Have the police and insurance people released the bakery?"

"No, not yet." I sat down on the bench and gazed at my bakery. My heart tightened, and a wave of nausea enveloped me. I leaned forward, pushing all thoughts of the chaos aside. "That's not why I'm calling."

"Okay, then, how can I help?"

"Josie gave me an idea, and I'm exploring the possibility since it will be months before I can reopen. But I need to find a contractor."

"What did you have in mind?"

"I have a small housekeeper's apartment off the kitchen. It seems to be the perfect setup to create a cottage kitchen where I can bake and sell items at a small stand outside my home. I just came from Elaine Snyder's office, and she'll be over at two to review the space. If she thinks the idea is viable, I will need someone to transform the area from a kitchen and dining space into a functional yet compact commercial kitchen."

He gave a low whistle. "I can meet you at two. I'm sure you'll want to get a couple of estimates, but I assure you my bid will be competitive. If you promise me a steady supply of that whole-wheat bread you make, we can get it done quickly."

"How long does it take to renovate a space?"

"Depending on what we find when we open the walls, three to six months."

I groaned at the thought of my house being in disarray all that time, but if I wanted to keep my business thriving, it would be a small price to pay. "Is there any chance we can keep it on the low end of the time frame?"

"What are your thoughts on sweat equity?"

"Um," I chuckled, "There's not a handy bone in my body."

"Can you haul debris to a dumpster and tidy up after a day of people working?"

"Sure."

"Okay, then we'll talk about what you can do to keep the job moving along, and we can set up a budget too. With your help, we can save some cost as well."

I perked up. "That would be a nice bonus—saving time and money."

"Then I'll see you at two o'clock."

I didn't need to give Russ my address since he had overseen work for Aunt Penny. "It's a plan."

Josie crossed the street, holding a cardboard tray with two cups and a bag. "Ready for a snack before the hospital?"

I patted the bench. "Yes, and I have good news."

She handed me the bag. "Sandwiches."

"Oh, you were thinking ahead, I'm starved."

She patted her belly and set the drink cups on the bench. "Thank my metabolism. I'm always hungry."

"I have the best news of the day. Russ Patterson will meet Elaine, you, and me, if you still want to be part of the fun, to discuss plans. Oh, and he mentioned that if I was willing to do some work like hauling debris and cleaning up after the workers, I could save some money, which might even speed up the completion time." My words faded as I noticed Gina, Louise, and Peter walking toward the burnt-out bakery.

Josie's gaze followed mine, her eyes narrowing. "What do you think they're doing?"

They walked around the edge of the building to the back. Although they didn't look up, they appeared to be focused on the foundation of the building.

"Searching for something." I pulled my sunglasses from my bag and put them on, along with a baseball cap I also had in there.

"What is that, a Mary Poppins bag?"

I handed Josie an extra pair of sunglasses. "During my training at the FBI, my shoulder bag contained everything I needed or wanted for the day, including snacks and an extra pair of socks. It was less stressful than needing something and not having it. Think of it like a high schooler's backpack, where they carry their world to school every day." I shrugged. "Some habits are hard to break."

12

———

"Is this what it's like to be undercover?" Josie asked.

"I never went undercover or on a stakeout, but I took a workshop. We're blending in with others who are enjoying the sunny day around lunchtime." I glanced at my watch. "We'll need to leave in ten minutes to get to the hospital."

"Any idea what they're looking for?"

"Your guess is as good as mine. If they're not careful, they might attract attention beyond just people relaxing on a bench."

Josie shifted on the seat for a clear view of the events unfolding across the street. "They don't seem to care who might see them. Couldn't that mean they have nothing to hide?"

"Criminals often show up at the scene of the crime they committed. Moths to a flame. It's irresistible. I wish I could walk over and ask what they're searching for."

"Why can't you? If they aren't doing anything illegal, they won't mind if you ask a question or two."

I tossed my half-eaten sandwich into the bag and stood up. "You're right. I own the property." While I waited at the crosswalk for the cars to stop, I kept the nosy-nellies in sight. With Josie beside me, we crossed, and I made a beeline for the pile of rubble. "Hello!"

Louise's head snapped up. "Temperance, I didn't expect to see you here."

"I was doing business at town hall and noticed you here. Are you looking for something?"

Gina slipped her arm around Louise's waist. "Since this is where Marty took his last breath, Louise wanted to pay her respects." Tears filled the woman's eyes.

Were they crocodile tears? "It looked like you were inspecting the foundation of the building."

Peter said, "Just being cautious not to step on broken glass or debris. You know, being extra careful."

He didn't need to repeat that. Was the man nervous because he was caught doing something other than what he claimed? "You probably shouldn't be over there. As far as I know, it's still an active crime scene." I pointed to the yellow tape fluttering in the light breeze. As the words left my lips, the sound of a car door shutting made me turn.

"Temperance. What's happening here?" Sergeant Franklin strode over. "This is an active crime scene."

"Josie and I were eating lunch across the street when I noticed Louise, Gina, and Peter over here. I was concerned for their safety; we came over to remind them it's not safe."

"Folks, Temperance is right—it's not."

"I apologize, Officer," Louise said, "I merely wanted to say goodbye to Marty."

Peter nodded. "Officer Butler said this is where Marty was found." His Adam's apple bobbed in his throat, and he looked away.

"As his girlfriend, you must understand I felt compelled to come here." Her eyes bore a pained expression as her hands clenched and unclenched.

Sergeant Franklin asked, "Do you know why he would break into the bakery?"

She shook her head. "He didn't like me working here, but he wasn't that angry. I never thought he'd be capable of committing a crime."

Gina said, "Most likely, he took Louise's key, broke in to vandalize the place, and got carried away."

"Would he have known where you kept your key?"

Louise nodded. "It stands out as it's the only purple one on my key ring."

"At some point, he must have taken it off and left her car keys. Then they had an argument, and she stormed off," Gina said. "It would have been easy enough for Louise to not realize it was gone since, most days, Temperance is usually at the bakery when we arrive. I know I don't give my key a second thought."

"She's right. I can't recall the last time, if ever, I arrived after the ladies."

Sergeant Franklin glanced at Peter. "Why are you here?"

Beads of sweat appeared on his forehead. "Being supportive of a friend."

"It's time for you to leave and do yourselves a favor—stay away from the area. I don't want to receive an emergency call that you've been injured."

His tone may have been gruff, but I agreed with him. Additionally, I wasn't sure if I could be held responsible. With the broken glass, shards of metal, wood, and heaven only knew, this place was a mess.

Tears slipped down Louise's cheek. "Can I have one final moment?"

When the sergeant didn't say no, she lowered her chin to her chest and closed her eyes. I noticed her lips moving, but she wasn't speaking aloud. Whatever it was, it brought more tears to her eyes. Was it regret?

Gina and Peter stood on either side of her, their arms

wrapped around her waist. After taking several deep breaths, she opened her eyes. "I'm finished."

They turned and walked down the alley.

"I'm glad you were driving by."

"We're keeping an eye on the scene. Something doesn't add up. I'm sure Butler mentioned that Martin Thompson didn't die from the fire."

Nodding, I said, "A blow to the head. Do you know if it was a tool or something else?"

Now that I had his full attention, he asked, "Why do you think it could have been a tool?"

"In the security footage, we see a person who appears to be Marty turning off the gas. When I took ownership of the building, I asked the gas company how to turn it off in case of an emergency, and they said I'd need to use a large wrench. At the end of the footage, we see someone throwing a wrench against the foundation out the back door. I assumed that's what it was."

Josie asked, "Could they have been looking for the wrench?"

"We have already entered it into evidence. Temperance, I know Butler has been keeping you updated on our progress, but we still have no leads on the identity of the second person. Our working theory is that Thompson broke in, got caught, somehow suffered a blow to the head, died, and the other person used the fire to cover up the murder."

"It still raises the question of why he was in the bakery at all. Someone took the master key from my kitchen a few weeks ago. Why now?"

"Do you keep some cash on the premises?"

"Nothing significant. As I mentioned earlier, a couple of hundred dollars, but not enough for Marty to break in and steal; besides he had a good-paying job."

"Sometimes criminals break in for the thrill that they can get."

Josie said, "But he didn't break in, a key was used."

I nodded. "Josie makes a good point." My phone rang. "Hold on for a moment." I stepped away to answer it.

"Hello."

"Doll, it's Celeste. Is everything okay? Jonah's worried about you since you're late, and we know you're never late. That bakery of yours opens at seven on the dot every single day."

I had no idea they kept such close track of my shop. "I'm sorry; I didn't mean to worry him. We're speaking with Sergeant Franklin, and I'll be there soon."

"Is there a break in the case? Does he know who hurt my sweetie?"

"Not yet. I know they're following every lead, but these things take time."

She sighed. "I understand, but you can't blame me for hoping."

"I do." It felt like I had repeated that sentiment too many times, even if only in my mind. "Josie and I are on our way. Do you need lunch?"

"No, I'm fine. Drive safely." She ended the call before I could say goodbye.

"Josie, that was Celeste. It seems Jonah's upset we're running late."

Sergeant Franklin said, "I'm sure they'll ask, but we still don't have any leads on his attacker. It's simply a matter of time."

"That's essentially what I just said to Celeste. I appreciate everything you are doing."

"Temperance, I hate to ask, but have you found anything? Your attention to detail in this situation could be invaluable."

Asking me must have been difficult for the sergeant. "Trust me. If I knew anything, you and Casey would be the first to know. No one wants these people caught more than me."

"All right. Be safe." He walked to his cruiser, his posture ramrod straight, but I knew the weight he bore. Although crime is complicated everywhere, Oak Hollow had seen two violent crimes in the last twenty-four hours.

"Come on, Josie. Let's visit Jonah and see what he remembers about the attack."

WE ARRIVED at the hospital at half past noon. Jonah was on the fourth floor, so we took the elevator up. Finding his room was easy because a police officer was still stationed outside. That sent a chill of fear through my veins. It meant he was still a target.

With forced smiles on our faces, Josie and I stopped at the door. "Temperance Matthews and Josie Shaw."

The officer nodded at us. "You're on the list."

I wondered who else was on the list, as the attacker could also be included if it was vague. I'd ask Casey about that later.

Jonah lay on his side, watching the door. Celeste sat beside the bed, holding his hand, every line on her face etched with concern. "Hi, Jonah, how are you feeling?"

Celeste said, "I'm happy you're here. He's been anxious to talk to you."

"We were delayed by a few stops, but we're here now." His face was pale and drawn. "Are you in pain?"

He closed his eyes as his breath shuddered. "It's not so bad."

I figured he was uncomfortable. "Can I get you anything?"

His eyes flew open and locked onto mine. "Justice."

"That's the job of the police."

He snorted. "You're smarter than anyone on that force,

which is why last night I came to see you. I never thought someone would attack me from behind."

Josie stood at the foot of his bed while I positioned myself between the bed and the door. "Did you have any idea you were being followed?"

"No. I told Officer Butler I've taken the shortcut many times, especially in my younger years. It never crossed my mind someone would use the thicket to lie in wait for me."

That was a great way to describe the area. Did the attacker know Jonah was headed to my place? I thought it but didn't ask; it was more likely that the person made an educated guess and followed him, waiting for the opportunity to strike. "Why were you coming to see me?"

His face scrunched up. "I remembered something important about the fire."

"That's great. Did you tell Officer Butler?"

Celeste patted his hand. "That's the problem. Jonah remembers he had to see you, but he doesn't remember what it was about. Only that he's convinced you're in danger."

A shiver of fear slid down my spine. One person was dead, another injured. Was I next? "From who started the fire?"

"I wish I knew. Dragging you over here is to remind you to stay vigilant."

"Thank you for letting me know." There had to be a way to bring out his memory. "Would you do an exercise with me?"

His eyes widened. "I'm not supposed to get out of bed without a nurse."

I patted the sheets. "Not that kind of exercise; this is about your memory."

He cast a worried glance at Celeste, and she nodded. "You have nothing to lose, sweetie."

In a gruff voice, he asked, "What do I need to do?"

Jonah trusted me. I swallowed the lump in my throat.

"Close your eyes and take several slow, deep breaths through your nose, then gently release the breath through your lips."

He did as I asked. On the fourth breath, I said, "With your eyes closed, I want you to picture yourself and Celeste walking down South Street. You're almost at Sassy's. Can you see the restaurant?"

With his eyes closed, he said, "Yes. I can see the OPEN sign and smell the basil in the air. It's a great way to lure people in for dinner."

"Do you see anyone you know?"

"I do. Alice, Peter, Erik Wool, and a few others maybe, I don't know."

"What happened next?"

He frowned. "Celeste had to drop an envelope in the mail. When I entered, Sassy's was packed and there were take-out orders stacked on top of the ovens."

"This is good, Jonah. What comes next?"

"I stood in line, and someone bumped into me. I turned around to ask them to wait their turn."

"Who was it?"

"I'm not sure," he said, opening his eyes. "People were standing in front of me, but I don't recall who they were."

"That's all right; don't put pressure on yourself. You'll remember when it's time."

He clenched his fist in the sheets. "It's maddening. I can almost see who was standing right in front of me. It slips in and out like a dream you can't quite remember."

I placed a comforting hand on his shoulder and said, "In due time. Is there anything else you wanted to tell me?"

"I talked to whoever it was. We chatted about your party."

This was recent news. "The picnic from a few weeks ago? Are you sure?"

"That's the only thing I remember. Temperance, I had to have seen or heard something I shouldn't have that day. I keep replaying the conversation as if it's on a loop."

Josie stepped closer to the bed, and my mouth went dry. "What do you remember, exactly?"

"It was at the picnic. We chatted about the food, the weather, and that you're a wonderful hostess. Then we started talking about the bakery, oh I remember Alice, Louise, and Gina were there."

I smiled. "Your memory *is* coming back." If only he'd mention the key again, but I wouldn't press him. That could be detrimental to him remembering.

His face brightened. "You did it." Then it drooped. "But who was I speaking to at Sassy's?"

Josie said, "Jonah, give it a little more time. With this breakthrough, I'm confident you'll remember the rest of the details soon."

Celeste asked, "Do you think what he remembered will help the investigation?"

"I'll tell Casey that he remembers the picnic. Even if it wasn't who he spoke to at Sassy's, it's a start. It narrows down the pool of suspects."

Jonah shifted, and Celeste hopped up to adjust the pillow behind his back. He said, "I guess any progress is helpful. I wanted to do more."

"You've experienced a significant shock to your body. Being stabbed, undergoing surgery, and your most important priority is recovery."

"Temperance, you're a wonderful person, and despite what's happened, I'm glad we sold the bakery to you. I feel terrible that this happened. Celeste will call as soon as I recall anything else."

"Don't forget the police are working on this case. You can contact either Sergeant Franklin or Officer Butler, as they're good at their jobs."

With an unblinking gaze, he said, "Sometimes in your life, you just have to follow your instincts about who is trustworthy and those you're less sure of. I'd trust you with my password list."

Pressing my hand to my heart, I smiled. "That's nice to hear, but I'm just an average baker."

He snorted. "Sure, and I'm a king."

Celeste kissed his forehead. "Sweetie, I'm going to walk the ladies down and get some coffee."

He closed his eyes. "I'm just going to hang out here."

I loved how Jonah maintained his sense of humor.

13

———

When we reached the hall, Celeste broke down in tears. I slipped my arm around her shoulder and steered her to a family waiting area.

She sniffled. "I'm sorry."

"Don't be." Josie knelt in front of her. "You've been through a lot in the last few hours. And it was scary as heck."

Celeste wiped her cheeks with the back of her hands. "I have to be strong for Jonah."

"That's why you're letting your emotions out with us." I glanced over my shoulder. "We're far enough away from the room for him to hear anything."

She stood. "I need to get a coffee. Otherwise, he'll suspect something."

"We'll walk with you." Josie nodded in agreement.

She shook her head. "No. I'm fine. You've got better things to do than watch me get a lousy cup of coffee."

"You never know. It might be the best cup you've ever had." I smiled, hoping that would lift her spirits.

We rode down the elevator together and stepped off on the main floor. She bobbed her head in the opposite direction of the exit. "Thanks for coming to see Jonah. Even though he didn't have a ton of specifics, I know it set his mind at ease."

"Our pleasure," I said. "If he remembers anything else, let me know." Before I took more than two steps, I turned. "Celeste, who's on the list to see Jonah?"

"Besides the hospital staff, the police, you, and Josie."

Nodding, I said, "Good. We'll check in later."

Josie waved. "Try to rest while Jonah's snoozing."

She gave us a half-hearted smile. "I will."

I watched her walk away. "Josie, whoever Jonah was talking to last night was likely the person who followed him, and they were at the picnic. Otherwise, there's no connection and Jonah's attack was a random act."

"That was my thought too, but if this is about patterns, who in that group, Alice, Peter, Gina, and Louise, would react on impulse?"

"We'll figure it out. We need to go back to when this was set in motion—the picnic."

Josie parked in my driveway, and I got out. Hank barked a happy greeting from the bay window.

"Now that's a warm welcome home," she laughed.

"We have about thirty minutes before Elaine and Russ arrive. You're staying?" I unlocked the door and pushed it open.

"Are you kidding? It will be the highlight of my day, watching my harebrained idea take shape, and stop asking. I'm all in!"

Hank bounded into the hall, barked, and wagged his tail, then raced into the dining room, around the table twice, zipped around the living room, and came back to the hall. Rolling onto his back, exposing his wiggling belly, he was ready for tickles and pets.

We had finished our sandwiches during the drive to the hospital, but I was still hungry. "How about coffee and cookies?"

My little pup trotted to the kitchen with a happy little wiggle in his backend.

"I shouldn't have said the C word. Now someone will think they're getting a treat."

As I suspected, Hank sat down, and his face transformed into the most adorable doggie smile. I dropped to my knees. "You're my little cookie monster, aren't you?"

"Woof!"

Josie took two mugs from the cabinet. "Regular or decaf?"

"Seriously?" I stood up and grabbed a few treats from the HANK canister.

She chuckled. "Regular it is, and it's nice that we agree on many topics, including coffee after the strangest twenty-four-plus hours ever."

"I'll grab my laptop. Be right back."

Calling after me, Josie said, "Could you grab mine? It's on top of my tote bag in the guest room."

I returned to the kitchen with our laptops, and we sat down with mugs of coffee while Hank curled up in his bed, snoring. "The printer's on." I interlaced my fingers and stretched, giving them a good wiggle. This was my way of transitioning my brain into my former work mode. Josie watched me closely.

"Part of your work ritual?"

Tipping my head back and then from side to side for a good stretch, I said, "Not one I use for baking, but yeah."

She mimicked my actions, and I chuckled. "Getting in the zone, super sleuth?"

Her smile was bright. "Something like that. Now, tell me what we're looking for."

I sipped my coffee, letting the ideas swirl around. "I'm not sure. There must be a connection to someone agreeing to help Marty and meet him at the bakery. If we knew who else wanted to vandalize the shop, it would narrow down who joined who."

"Should we assume Marty went there to vandalize the place? Perhaps not to burn it down, but to shut it down for a couple of weeks, forcing Louise to find a new job."

"And Louise followed him after she discovered his plan?"

"She wanted to stop him." I leaned forward and typed Louise Fletcher into the search bar. "Can you look up Alice and Peter? Avoid social media to start. Check for sites that show locations and list basic information. Take a screenshot of what you find. I'll do the same with Marty, Louise, and Gina."

"What are you looking for?"

"If they ever crossed paths before living in Oak Hollow. There's a dotted line to here. Louise and Gina aren't local. When you are done, print your notes. It will make it easier to compare. If Peter and Louise dated previously, it was before she moved to town since the entire time she's lived with Marty."

We spent the next half hour in silence, broken only by the soft clinks of coffee cups placed on the table as we sipped, refilled, and sipped again.

"How's it going?" she asked.

I looked up from my screen. "I have a lot of pages to print. Marty and Louise moved frequently, and from my search results, Gina may have crossed paths with them a couple of years ago in Cave Spring, Georgia, a small town with a charming bakery. It seems like the kind of place that would attract an up-and-coming baker, and it is about ninety minutes outside of Atlanta near the Appalachian Trail."

"Is that significant?"

"Gina loves to hike. When I first hired her, she peppered me with questions about the best hiking spots in the area. She loves adventure, camping, and all that goes with it."

Josie half closed her laptop. "That means she's comfortable in the woods?"

"Sure, why is that important?"

"A sweatshirt was discovered near the pond in the woods."

"Casey never confirmed it was Louise's. Anyone could have dropped it."

"What if person two dropped it to redirect suspicion toward Louise, and what if person two is Gina? Being in the woods at night wouldn't bother her."

"They're friends. Why would she want to frame Louise?" *However, Josie had a point, sort of.* "Remember, it rained; anyone could have dropped it twenty-four hours prior to the fire. It wasn't soaked or covered in mud. Therefore, it was an educated conclusion that it belonged to person two." I tapped a message to Casey. *Was there any evidence found on the hoodie?*

"What about Alice and Peter? Did they ever live in Georgia?"

She pursed her lips. "No, they have always lived in Massachusetts. They both attended Mill River High School. Peter grew up in the next town, and Alice moved here four years ago."

"That was before Marty and Louise moved to the area three years ago. Could Peter have dated Louise in high school?"

"Good question. I need to see where Louise attended school."

She pursed her lips. "When did Gina move here?"

"Six months before I opened the bakery. Does this indicate that Gina followed them, and why didn't they mention knowing each other prior to working at the bakery?" I locked eyes with Josie. "We need to talk to the ladies and investigate their past. What were they hiding? I wouldn't have cared if they knew each other before hiring them. Friends working together can create a stronger team."

She grinned. "Like us."

I smacked my hand on the table and grinned, "Exactly."

Hank gave a sharp bark, his tail thumping against the cushion. "Yes, sweet baby, you too."

A knock on the door made me glance at my clock and lean back. "Time for the little bakery discussion."

Josie got up and unlocked the apartment door from the kitchen, where I greeted Elaine and Russ in front.

"Please come in and thank you for coming over so quickly."

Elaine smiled at Russ and then at me. "I see that you're ready to get started."

"Idle hands and all that." I pointed to the kitchen. "We can enter the apartment through the kitchen."

Elaine poked her head into the living and dining rooms. "Your home is lovely."

"Thank you, but I can't take credit for it. Aunt Penny decorated it, and it suits me. Aside from a few personal items, it's her signature style, not mine. I must say up front that the apartment is outdated, so I don't mind renovating it."

Josie was in the apartment when Elaine walked in first. Russ had me walk ahead of him, and when we were inside, he looked around, nodding.

Elaine asked, "Tell me your vision?"

I crossed the room and stood by the back door. "I thought we'd gut the kitchen and living room space. Adding a central stainless steel island in the middle. Two sets of wall convection ovens, a dishwasher, refrigerator, and freezers would be on this wall. Open shelves for storage on the living room wall. Along with a bread-rising area over here."

"Of course, you're gutting to the studs and rebuilding." She circled the space. "Double sink?"

"Yes. Stainless steel. All appliances will be commercial grade."

She tapped her pen to her lips, "You'll have to upgrade the water heater. Also, you'll need an electrical upgrade and a gas line for the equipment. With the apartment being outdated, I'm sure the systems are the same age."

"I have natural gas now." The dollars were adding up at an alarming rate.

Russ stated, "That's simple enough to verify for sufficient supply."

"And the floor?" Elaine asked as she jotted down notes.

"Under the carpet is solid oak flooring. One idea I had was to sand and seal it with epoxy. I had a germ-resistant epoxy-covered cement floor in the bakery." I looked at Russ. "If possible, I want to explore sealing the wood and keeping its natural appearance."

Elaine nodded. "If you can provide documentation that it's sanitary, like tile or cement flooring, I'll sign off on it."

He said, "Most epoxy floors are safer than kitchen tiles. Adding texture provides a good grip."

My breath came in quick and shallow gasps. *The floor. Did that contribute to the spread of the fire?*

"Temperance, if you drop off the permit application tomorrow, I'll process it immediately. Once your contractor is ready, you could begin demolition." She stuck out her hand. "I'm excited for this new chapter."

"Thank you, Elaine. I appreciate your support."

"Just doing my job, and we don't want the town to be without your delicious baked goods for too long. Can you show me where you plan to install the bakery stand out front?"

Russ asked, "Do you mind if I poke around the basement to see what we might need for system upgrades?"

"Not at all. I'll be right back." I opened the back door to show Elaine how I would get the product from the new kitchen to the stand.

"As you can see, the driveway is asphalt, so a rack will easily roll to the sidewalk." I hurried to the spot I had in mind. "In the back of the garage, I have an old flat wagon on iron wheels. Picture an oversized flower cart with a roof and open shelves on the bottom and top. It would be stocked with loaves of bread, muffins, and cookies. There would be a lockbox, and sales would be on the honor system."

She gave me a side-eye. "Don't you think that's pretty trusting for a woman whose business was destroyed by criminals?"

"I'll have a camera system to monitor for theft. But I can't let the fire alter my faith in people."

A small smile warmed her eyes. "I agree, but you surprise me. Do you think you'd have pies or cakes?"

"In all honesty, I haven't thought that far ahead. Gina did the sweet baking. I took care of the savory items. The space will be large enough for two people to work. I don't know what her plans will be. Maybe she'll want to take some extended time away from baking."

Elaine pushed her sunglasses up her nose. "Louise has had quite a shock. It wouldn't surprise me if those two did some traveling together."

I gave her a sharp look. "Why do you say that?"

"Last week, when I was in the bakery, they were chatting about a long overdue road trip out west. Do you know how some people are living the van life? I got the impression that's what they were talking about."

"I've heard about people giving up their homes to live on the road, but I wasn't aware they were interested in that lifestyle." I'd have to ask Josie if she ever heard them talking about a western adventure. "Maybe a change of pace would be good for them after what's happened, and by the time I reopen the old location, they'll be back."

"A sabbatical. I'm sure they can collect unemployment." Her phone chirped. "Oh, that's my alarm. I need to run. I have another appointment in fifteen minutes. Be sure to get the paperwork in tomorrow, and I'll move it along."

"Thanks, Elaine." My footsteps were slow as I walked to

the apartment entrance. Was the timing of Gina and Louise discussing a road trip coincidence? I shook my head. Not possible. Could Louise have provoked Marty to vandalize the shop to escape a terrible relationship? Once he was caught, she'd be free to do or go anywhere she pleased—two birds, one stone.

I climbed the steps to the back door. It would be better to have a ramp for deliveries. "Russ?" I called out.

Josie held a yellow legal pad and was writing.

"Can you add a widened door and ramp and refurbish the wagon to the list?"

She nodded. "What else did you think of?"

"Off topic, make a new list. Gina and Louise, road trip. How long have they been friends, and why did Gina move to Oak Hollow? Was it because Louise and Marty lived here?"

Josie's eyes widened. "What did Elaine share?"

My eyebrow arched, and I crossed my arms over my chest. "Gina and Louise were discussing a van adventure out west without mentioning Marty going with them."

Her eyes widened. "You're kidding."

"We may have found a motive." I narrowed my eyes. "Before we track them down for this conversation, I want to scour their social media accounts and see how far back their friendship goes. There's a link we haven't explored yet."

14

"Hey Louise, it's Temperance."

"Hello." She sounded upbeat.

"Would you mind if Josie and I stopped over at Gina's? We wanted to see how you're doing. I've made banana nut muffins."

"Those are my favorites. Did you add a sprinkle of mini chocolate chips, too?"

"Is there any other way?" I forced the smile into my voice.

She laughed. "Stop by anytime. We're just chilling on the porch, drinking coffee, and talking about the future."

"See you soon." Disconnecting, I said, "Josie, you're never going to believe this. Louise said she and Gina are talking about their future. Our timing might be perfect."

Rubbing her hands together, she said, "This should be very interesting."

I frowned. "What about your job? All you've done today is go with me to town hall, see Jonah, deal with the new kitchen, and now this."

She lifted her shoulder and shrugged. "I'm between gigs."

"Doubtful. You're a talented graphic artist. I'm sure you have lots of contracts for design work."

"The beauty of working for myself is I set my schedule. To be creative, I need to take breaks. This happens to be a scheduled week off. Which I plan every two months."

Tipping my head, I said, "Are you sure?" My words came out more like a drawl.

She held her palm up. "Honest."

The oven timer dinged. "My excuse is ready."

Once I packed the bakery box, we drove across town to Gina's place. I parked next to the sidewalk, and just as Louise had said, she and Gina were in the same seats they'd occupied yesterday when we stopped by with Casey. I said, "Showtime," just loud enough for Josie to hear.

When Louise saw us, she stood and waved. Her face was relaxed. Not at all what I expected with her boyfriend dying yesterday. She didn't have guilt written over it either. We climbed the porch steps.

"Temperance, this is so sweet of you. Stopping by to check on us. We should be consoling you as well."

Gina said, "Any news yet?"

So much for pleasantries. "Not that the police have told me. We went and saw Jonah earlier, and he's going to make a full recovery."

Gina exhaled. "What a relief. Does he know who attacked him?"

"Sadly, no. His memory's gone, and it might be permanent. There's no way to tell."

Thankfully, Josie didn't contradict my statement. We never discussed if his memory loss would be temporary, and of course, there was every reason to believe it wouldn't since it was already coming back a little at a time.

"That's too bad. About his memory." Louise said, "At least

physically, he'll be okay. He's such a nice man, and Celeste, too."

"They are." I held out the box. "Still warm from the oven."

Gina got up. "I'll get coffee."

Josie said, "I'll help you."

She went inside with Gina, allowing me to speak with Louise. Once the door closed, I sat in a chair across from her. "How are you feeling? You've suffered quite a shock."

"I have my moments, but Gina's been a rock. I couldn't ask for a better friend."

My opening. "Have you been friends for a long time?"

"Since we were little. We lost touch for years, but then, out of the blue, we bumped into each other in this cute little town in Georgia. Marty and I had taken a year off after college and were bumming around. That was about six months before he got the job in Oak Hollow. Then, in a happy twist of fate, Gina moved to town right before you opened Early Rise. She wanted to be closer to me. With her skills, she hoped you'd hire her. Then you hired me too, but we weren't sure you'd approve. I'm sorry we kept our friendship from you. But no harm, right?"

"No harm done. Amazing how life works out."

She beamed. "I'm lucky." Her smile dimmed. She was like a seesaw. "Then, when things got rocky between Marty and me, she was my sounding board. He wanted me to do more than work in someone else's business. Gina's always encouraged me to do what I wanted to do."

"Did you want to do something different?"

"No. I liked working for you. I'm still trying to find my passion."

"You're fortunate to have reconnected with Gina after all those years apart."

Josie held the door for Gina, carrying a tray. "Here we go." She set it down on the small rectangular table. "What have you been chatting about while coffee was brewing?" She glanced at Louise but gave me a hard look.

Louise said, "Our friendship and how lucky I am."

Gina squeezed her shoulder and smiled. "We both are."

I took the mug Gina handed me. "Checking on Louise was just one reason I wanted to stop by. I have news about the bakery and my plans."

Louise and Gina exchanged a fleeting glance, with Gina biting her lower lip. "I can't wait to hear," she said.

I took a moment. Even though I had a plan, this was still hard on me. "Since the bakery is a total loss, and there's so much to do once the insurance company releases funds to clear the site and rebuild, I've decided to open a little bakery."

I let the words sink in before continuing. "I've had the building inspector and Russ Patterson, from RP Contracting, evaluate the apartment attached to my house. I plan to renovate the kitchen and living space and convert it into a commercial kitchen. Then, I'll sell the baked goods from an old-fashioned flower cart in front of my place."

"Wow. That wasn't what I expected to hear." Gina didn't look at me or anyone but stared at her mug. "Why aren't you waiting to reopen the bakery? It won't take long, will it?"

"It could take up to eighteen months or longer if we run into delays. That's a huge risk to my customer base. I've worked hard to build a steady clientele for my breads and other items since I opened."

Louise's voice trembled. "Does that mean you'll need Gina to make cakes but not me?"

"The kitchen will be large enough for two people to work simultaneously, but I'm going to evaluate my best sellers and start there."

"Who cares, Louise? We can collect unemployment benefits for a while." Gina's gaze darted between me and Josie. "Right?"

Nodding I said, "Yes. You can."

Louise gave me a somber look. "It might be good to take a break after all that's happened."

Josie said, "Have you completely recovered from the diabetic issue?"

"After all these years, this was the easiest recovery. I'm sure it was the hospital stay and, of course, being pampered by Gina, plus everyone's been so kind. You and Temperance especially. Then we met with Alice and Peter last night in town."

Gina said, "Yeah, Peter noticed you were waiting to pick up your pizza."

"There's nothing like comfort food after a stressful event," Josie said.

I noticed Gina's tone had a hostile edge. Was she being overprotective of Louise? Most likely. It's what I'd do for Josie if I thought someone was poking at her. However, I needed to dig deeper into her night in the woods.

"It could have been so much worse if you hadn't found your way to my house before collapsing. Who knows what would have happened."

"She wears a watch with the location turned on. I would have used that to find her if I hadn't heard from her."

Tension crackled the air. "That's smart. Sadly, the world we live in, you can't be too careful," I said.

"These muffins are delicious." Louise buttered two halves and handed a piece to Gina. "Just the right amount of choco-late to nut ratio."

"I'm glad you're enjoying them." Over the rim of my coffee mug, I looked at Josie and glanced at Louise, hoping she'd pick up on my prodding so she could keep talking. I was sure I had annoyed Gina about Louise getting lost in the woods.

Josie said, "Temperance, while the construction is ongo-ing, maybe you should take a vacation. Go to the beach and soak up some rays. Once you reopen, establishing your business will keep you busy."

Louise said, "A vacation sounds like heaven. I've always wanted to experience life on the open road—driving where I want and seeing all the great places in the country's western half. When Marty and I first got together, we did that in the southeast, and it was amazing."

Josie leaned forward. "I didn't know you'd traveled like that. Did you have a motorhome or travel trailer?" She glanced at me. "That must have been so romantic, just the two of you and nothing but blacktop in front of you."

She laughed. "You make it sound more romantic than it was. At times, Marty could be a bit of a drag. Every few weeks, we had to get jobs; we'd pick a town, stay for a while, and work before taking off again, living like nomads."

Gina said, "Actually, that's how Louise and I bumped into each other again. I was living in Georgia, outside of Atlanta, and they rolled into town and walked into the café where I was working."

"Stop being modest, Gina. It wasn't a little café. It was also a bakery, and you worked your magic there too."

Color flushed Gina's cheeks. That was a new look for her. I'd never seen her blush. "She's right. You're a talented baker."

"Thanks, Temperance. I'm just sorry we won't be working together for the foreseeable future. Louise is right; we all should take a vacation and regain our equilibrium."

Setting her mug aside, Josie crossed her legs, "If you could go anywhere, where would it be?"

Gina placed her fingertips on her chest. "Me?"

Josie nodded. "We'll go around the group. It'll be fun."

Louise said, "I'd go out west. I've always wanted to visit the national parks and the redwoods. I've heard they're spectacular."

I said, "An island where I wouldn't have to leave a lounge

for a week except to shower and go to a fabulous restaurant for dinner. Josie, I've got a chair right next to me with your name on it."

"Sounds like heaven, but let's say two weeks. We can't completely unwind in seven days." She chuckled. "What about you, Gina, a luxury resort, dude ranch, or wait, you enjoy hiking, don't you?"

"I'm with Louise on this. In fact, I've never been past the Mississippi River. If Louise would have me, I'd tag along. There are great state parks and lots of hiking, which would be perfect."

"We'll need a van." Louise snapped her fingers. "Wait a sec, we could retrofit Marty's truck." Her face fell. "That sounded cold, like I don't care he's dead." She rubbed the back of her neck, and her breathing was ragged. "I might as well confess."

My heartbeat slowed. Was she about to say she was involved with his death? "You can confide in us."

Gina hissed, "What are you doing?"

"It'll be okay. The truth is bound to come out eventually. I might as well tell Temperance and Josie first. They've been so nice through this mess." She cleared her throat. "Right before I left the house after fighting with Marty for what seemed like hours, I screamed, *I wished he was dead*. I was tired of the fighting and wanted out."

I reached over and placed my hand on hers. "Saying it in anger doesn't make it happen. You can't curse someone."

She stared at the floor. "I know, but our relationship ended that night. All the fights about me not living up to my potential was too much of a burden. He wanted me to quit the bakery, but I loved working there, and Gina and I got to spend every day together. Just like when we were kids."

I wouldn't mention Louise and Marty seemed very much in love in the pictures from the party. "Gina, how did you feel about Marty pressuring Louise to get a different job?"

Her eyes narrowed. "He wanted to control everything she did, and he knew I was team Louise all the way. Needless to say, we used to butt heads."

"That's why I told Marty I was done and stormed out. After I calmed down, I knew I could stay at Gina's for a couple of nights until I decided what to do next."

I asked, "Then why didn't you come here right away instead of sitting by the pond all night?"

"I tried to call, but you didn't answer the first time. I thought about leaving town to clear my head, but I wanted my things. I only took enough for a couple of days." Her chin quivered. "Marty and I could have talked and come to an arrangement where I could stay at the house for a while."

This statement conflicted with what she said yesterday: they would have made up. Casey would want to hear this information. Did she think she could be more forthcoming with us because she considered us friends?

Gina said, "None of that matters now. Besides, I'm sure his family won't give you his truck, so we'll figure it out."

She slumped back in the chair. "You're right, but I should get something from that toxic relationship."

How could their relationship have soured in three weeks, from my party to now? "What kind of an arrangement were you going to talk with him about?"

"I put a lot of money into that house he bought, and he needed to reimburse me. We split all the bills, so technically, I helped pay the mortgage."

Gina patted her arm. "You don't need to think about that now, Louise. You can stay with me for as long as you like."

"When will the police let me in so I can get the rest of my things, or better yet, I can move back in?" She looked from Josie to me. "Would you put in a good word with Officer Butler for me?"

"I can mention to her and Sergeant Franklin that you were asking, but you can do that too. It's your legal address, and

I'm not clear on the laws regarding occupancy if Marty owned the house. You aren't on the mortgage?"

She shook her head. "I wish. My credit wasn't that great when he bought the place. Even with it being a fixer-upper, it was still expensive."

Josie said, "At the very least, they'll let you pack your things."

I set the mug aside. "If I speak with anyone at the department, I'll let them know you have questions."

She leaned over, hugged me, and gave me a broad smile. "Thanks for stopping by today and for the muffins."

Josie did a double take. I felt as if we had just been dismissed. I got to my feet. "If you need anything, give Josie or me a call."

"That's much appreciated. If you could talk to the police about getting in my house, that would be best."

Surprised at her insistence, I wondered, did she think I had sway with the local PD? "Sure. I'll see what I can do."

Gina said, "You should take that beach vacation you mentioned. We're going to give our western adventure serious consideration."

Louise nodded. "Take care and drive safely on the way home." She walked me down the steps to the car.

Once I got in and buckled up, I looked at her. She waved and slipped her hands in her pockets as she ran up the steps.

Josie said, "I guess we overstayed our welcome. Did you feel like we were just hustled out the door, as if they couldn't wait to get rid of us?"

I nodded and pulled away from the curb. "What did I say that made them abruptly change their demeanor? Also, I wanted to ask why they seemed so happy at the picnic. I find that very odd indeed."

"Agreed. What if Louise's endgame is to use you to get back into the house? She was being excessively chatty, and then Gina mentioned taking a trip. I find it all off-putting. If

Louise had fallen out of love with Marty, she would seem okay that he died, less of a complication, and there wouldn't have been any problematic conversation saying she was leaving town either."

With a glance in my rearview, I said, "One thing's for sure, with the two of them watching us leave, they were ready to end all conversation with us." I flicked on my blinker and turned the corner, relieved to no longer be watched.

15

———————

$\mathcal{J}$osie drove home, leaving me to wander around the kitchen while making a quick pot of chili. Clearing my thoughts always helped put data into perspective. I experienced so many emotions today. Planning for the future felt rewarding, and I'd start emptying the apartment tomorrow. Seeing Jonah recover was a relief, but talking with Louise and Gina solidified my original instinct that one or both were hiding something. If that hoodie could be connected to Louise, it could be the link needed to solve Marty's murder.

"Hank, what if…" He barked twice as if ready to consult on the case.

"That's right. We're going to mull over ideas." He barked again and wagged his tail as fast as he could.

Chopping an onion, I said, "Two people entered the bakery in the wee hours of the morning. One turned off the gas, one set a fire, and only one person left the building alive. We have two strong suspects for person two. Louise and Gina. But what about Peter or even Alice? Celeste told us that Alice mentioned seeing Jonah before the attack. What about that knife? Were fingerprints on the handle, and what kind of knife was it? It was small, which isn't enough of a descriptor. Those are questions for Casey."

I turned the pot on, drizzled in olive oil, placed the onions in, peeled the garlic, and ran it through the press before adding it to the pot with diced yellow bell peppers. Tilting my head, I picked up the paring knife I had just used and turned it over in my hands, feeling its weight. Holding it as if I were about to stab a human being, I walked into my office for a ruler and measured the blade. "Two and one-half inches." Could a similar knife have been used to stab Jonah?

"A paring knife would have been easy to swipe from the pizza shop. Who had Jonah seen there, or what did he realize?" I returned to the chili pot and stirred before adding the ground meat.

Several minutes passed. I kept going back to Celeste. "She said Alice mentioned Jonah was going toward my house. But how would she know that if she had only seen Jonah walk out of Sassy's? Did he mention where he was going?"

Woof!

"Do you like my spinning ideas? How about this: Alice and Peter were with Louise and Gina."

What was it about the four of them? "Hank, we need to look at the picnic pictures again. This time, examining each one from corner to corner. I feel like I've overlooked an important detail."

He lay down, eyelids heavy, bored with my conversation. Before I covered my pot, I stirred in the spices, set the burner to simmer and set the timer for fifteen minutes. My computer was still on the kitchen table.

I scrolled through the images of the food and stopped to study the candid photos of my guests. There was one picture of Josie with Celeste and Jonah, and I blew up the outer edge. "Well, hello there. Alice and Marty arguing; their pinched expressions showed it was a heated exchange, although the photo is a little fuzzy."

A few pictures later, Marty was with Louise, and her face was pinched, eyes narrowed. It's too bad this wasn't a video, and I could read their lips if I couldn't hear what they were saying." A few more pictures later, Louise seemed to slip something to Alice while Gina hovered close. "Why hadn't I noticed this nonsense during the party?"

Talking to myself didn't yield answers. However, I needed a sounding board. My first thought was Celeste. She might have noticed what was happening since she'd been at the picnic. Clearly, Jonah had, but I didn't want to impose any extra pressure on his recovery. For his memory to return, it needed to happen when his body and mind were ready to accept the truth. Casey was the logical choice since Josie had been with me since this mess started, and we'd discussed these details to death. I needed a fresh perspective.

I called before I could second guess myself.

"Butler."

"Hi, Casey. It's Temperance Matthews."

"Hello. Is everything all right?"

"Yes." I paused. "I've been mulling over the case, and I was wondering if you had some time, maybe when you take your dinner break, to discuss a few details that are bugging me."

"I'm not on duty tonight. The captain insisted I take the night off. I've been clocking too many hours over the last few days. I can swing by your place anytime."

"You're welcome to have dinner with me if you're interested. There's a pot of chili simmering on my stove."

"That sounds delicious. What time?"

"Anytime, and come around to the kitchen door."

"Can do. Thirty minutes?"

"Perfect. See you then."

After setting my phone aside, I whipped up a pan of cornbread, slid that into the oven, and stirred in the last chili ingredients. There was enough time to print out the additional photos for Casey to take with her.

I followed the timeline as I thought it occurred. Marty decided to enter my bakery and create havoc; the plan started at or around the time of my party. Could it be as simple as he was trying to force Louise to quit her job? It was a silly excuse to set fire to a building.

A tap on the glass had me glance up and wave Casey inside.

She held up a six-pack of Dashton Brewery pale ale. "Since we saw this a few times over the last two days, I thought we might try it."

"I'll get frozen mugs."

She nodded. "Fancy. I like it."

"Not really. I can't stand warm beer." She took two bottles from the pack while I slid the rest into the fridge. "I printed some photos to discuss, but first, can we go over my ideas? Maybe you can confirm some details if it doesn't break confidentiality."

"What am I looking at?" She flipped through the stack of photos.

"Focus on the small things on the periphery of the images. But first the knife was used to stab Jonah was a paring knife."

Her brow quirked a fraction of an inch. "How did you deduce that?"

I held up my knife. "It's the right length, easy to steal from, say, Sassy's Pizzeria and it would be small enough to hide while stalking the intended victim."

"I believe it came from there."

"Fingerprints?" I asked.

She shook her head. "No. There were bits of garlic peel at the base of the blade."

More to myself I said, "The assailant took it from Sassy's."

"Did Jonah have anything new when you saw him?"

"Nothing earth-shattering. His memory is coming back,

and it's just a matter of time before he remembers the attack. He said someone jostled him at Sassy's, but he can't remember who."

I gestured for Casey to have a seat at the table. She said, "He recalls that Alice, Erik Wool, and Peter were there. Erik was picking up a pizza, and I've confirmed that he was on duty at the firehouse."

"Really, Jonah talked with me about the picnic. I wonder if he could have confused the two events. But it's interesting about Erik, he hasn't pinged my radar. Maybe he should have; he was at the picnic, the fire, and Sassy's."

"It's a small town, Temperance. We tend to see the same people over and over again."

"Unless they came into the bakery, I never saw anyone."

With a laugh, she said, "That's because all you did was work. The only reason I know the habits of so many locals is I see people on patrol. If I were working in a kitchen like you, I wouldn't either."

I sipped my beer, "I've uncovered a few details today that you might find interesting." I waited for her to ask what. When she didn't but instead gave me a contemplative look, I added, "Gina and Louise have been friends since childhood and lived in the same small town in Georgia before relocating here."

"I don't understand the relevance."

"When I hired them at the bakery, neither said a word about knowing the other. When Elaine Snyder inspected the apartment—I'm converting into a commercial kitchen—she mentioned that just last week, Gina and Louise discussed taking an extended trip out west."

Her irises flickered. "Interesting."

"Josie and I did a little digging and put the pieces together that they knew each other before moving to Oak Hollow. I wanted to know how well so we took a box of muffins to Gina's."

She smiled. "To check on Louise?"

"Of course. I told them about the little bakery I'm starting while waiting for the brick-and-mortar version to be replaced, and in conversation, they volunteered that Louise and Marty used to live like nomads. She always wanted to do the western swing of the country. That's when they encouraged me to take a vacation. They kept talking about where they'd go on the trip since they'd get unemployment checks." I held up a finger. "Wait for this. Louise wanted to take Marty's truck, do some work on it, and use that as the travel vehicle."

"Huh. Where did Elaine say she was when she overheard the conversation?"

"Last week in the bakery. Oh, and you know how we thought, well I thought, the beer mugs in the sink couldn't have been from Louise and Marty because of the sugar content in beer?"

"You were wrong?"

"If she drinks beer, she eats to balance the carbs."

"This is circumstantial evidence, but I like how the pieces fit together."

I wiped condensation from my mug. "A pattern."

Casey crossed one leg over the other and drummed her short fingernails against the tabletop. "If I understand you correctly, you believe Louise is responsible for Marty's death?"

"They're of similar height and build." I slid the photo of them from the picnic across the table.

She took a look. "Do you think he went to the bakery, she followed him, and they got into another argument?"

"I do, and it all ties back to Marty wanting Louise to quit her job."

"At some time after the picnic, he takes her key. They fight. Louise storms out; he goes to the bakery, intent on vandalizing, which is why he turns off the gas before entering through the back door. Wait, that's not possible."

Jumping up, I circled the table and took my keys from my purse. "He couldn't have entered through the back door with Louise's key. Remember, there are four masters: mine, one in my safe, Josie's copy, and the spare hanging on the back door. Someone used my spare master key, and when Louise mentioned he must have taken her key, saying it was the colored one on the ring, why wouldn't she say the purple key? The master is pink, but maybe she didn't realize that tidbit was important, or she was trying to misdirect me."

"That's an excellent point about the colors. Did he get the key at the party?"

I rummaged through the papers and found the image of Alice and Louise. "Look at this. What if Alice took it and passed it to Louise, and she went to the bakery first? Marty followed her, they argued, she pushed him, and he died. We only have her word she was at the pond thinking, but she could have been horrified at what she'd done and ran."

Casey studied the image. "What else do you have?"

"Alice and Marty arguing." I handed her the next image. "Look closely. Those faces aren't engaged in friendly banter."

Her brow arched. "And the hoodie?"

"You said yourself it wasn't rain soaked or caked with mud. It wasn't there long."

Casey set the image aside. "Evidence is mounting against Louise, but it's still circumstantial. Can we place her at Sassy's when Jonah was there?"

"No, but maybe that's what he's blocking. Louise had just lost her partner in the fire." I threw my arms in the air. "Let's not forget neither Louise nor Gina shed a tear when you provided the death notification."

"True." She dragged the word out. "That doesn't mean she's guilty. I've witnessed many different reactions when informing someone their loved one has passed. She had been through her trauma, going to the hospital close to a diabetic coma."

That was a good point. "I can't dismiss that Louise was a sick woman. However, if you had diabetes all your life, wouldn't you carry those emergency gel packs in your pockets at all times?"

"Yes, but I can't judge anyone by my yardstick of being overly prepared."

I sat on the corner of the table. "There was a wrench, right? Did it come from a set belonging to Marty?"

Hesitating, she said, "No. It was recently purchased. The teeth were pristine. If someone had used it, there would have been some wear on the teeth." She narrowed her gaze. "For the record, I didn't tell you, you guessed."

"Gotcha. Did Sergeant Franklin mention we saw Gina, Louise, and Peter searching the perimeter of the bakery? Peter said they were keeping an eye on the ground to avoid broken glass so Louise could pay respect to Marty, where he died."

"Huh, that's different."

"Franklin told them to steer clear; it wasn't safe, and it was still an active crime scene."

"Good for him. He keeps to the letter of the law, and I like that."

"When I asked the sergeant about Marty's head wound, after the others were gone, he wouldn't confirm it was a wrench."

"The medical examiner theorized he hit his head on the oven door handle. The possibility exists that he tripped and fell into the stove or that someone pushed him.

"Then why toss the wrench out the back door? If that's what Louise and her friends were looking for?"

"You said they were looking at the foundation. Wouldn't they have looked closer to the back door if they wanted to find the wrench?"

"Could the force of the water from the fire hose push it aside?"

"I like the way your brain pivots, Temperance. It's easy to

see how you were good at your old job. And it's possible. Water is powerful, and the force of the water could have washed the wrench away from the door. It's like your hose washing dirt from your car."

"As much as I wish this weren't true, it looks like Louise was in her car regrouping after the quarrel. If she didn't go into the bakery first, she saw Marty sneak down the street and slip inside. The argument continued. She shoved him and then set fire to the shop to cover up his death. Then guilt overwhelmed her, and she took off into the woods." I narrowed my eyes. "We know Marty parked his vehicle at his job which is a ten-minute drive so he didn't walk to the bakery."

Casey leaned against the table. "What are you thinking?"

"What if he had an accomplice from the beginning? Person number two might have gotten antsy thinking he was taking too long, and they went inside to see what the delay was. Was that person Louise? It'd explain why her car was parked on the street."

"But her burning the bakery doesn't fit with any working theory. Unless you have another idea."

I nodded. "Or I have several."

16

———

*O*ver bowls of spicy chili and cornbread, Casey and I pushed theories to the point where I could no longer distinguish between real or impossible. My eyes burned, and my back ached. I needed a hot bath and a good night's rest.

She stared at the window. "I don't believe you were the target but a tool for lashing out. The argument confirmed Marty was angry with Louise. Without knowing the identity of person two, we can't uncover the truth. If any of your ideas are correct, it could be Louise, Peter, or even Gina."

"The hoodie found near the pond didn't yield anything?"

"No. I wonder if someone planted it there to lead us to Louise."

"She's my strongest suspect. I know they've been together for years, and all couples argue, but what's different about this time? She packed her things and left for at least overnight, if not for a couple of days."

Casey picked up her empty dishes and stood. "We're not making any progress. You're exhausted, and I need sleep. My superpower of staying awake needs a recharge."

I smiled. "Are there other abilities I should know about?"

Laughing, she said, "An overwhelming desire to catch the

bad guy. Not that we have much crime in town, but when we do, I'm prepared with handcuffs and an uncomfortable ride to the station."

"I'll bear that in mind." We walked to the back door, and I turned on the floodlight. "I'm glad you stopped by. Even if we didn't solve the case, we discussed many theories, and within them lay the truth."

"We have to wait for Jonah to regain his memory. Whoever tried to prevent him from speaking with you had something important to conceal."

I nodded. "The fire and death of Marty."

She nodded to the apartment door. "It's great to hear that you're pivoting with the bakery. You're going to do great."

"I hope so. Building a business from the ground up or, in this case, from the floorboards comes with additional expense, but I can't sit around twiddling my thumbs. I'd go stir crazy."

"You wouldn't consider going back to the FBI?"

"No. That's my past. Small-town life has grown on me, and I've made a few friends. Living in Virginia, all I had was work, co-workers, baking, and feeding said co-workers. I want more out of life."

Casey looked across the driveway. "I'd like to think we're becoming friends. Can I say something that might be too personal or oversteps a boundary?"

"In my book, genuine friends speak the truth but do so with kindness."

"I know you have Josie as a good friend and confidant. You also spend every day at the bakery, working from before sunrise until late afternoon. Did you create a new life, or did you trade one closed-off existence for another?" She held up her hand. "You don't need to answer, but consider your new venture. It's on a smaller scale, and if it works for you financially, it might provide the balance you've been seeking."

"Hmm. I hadn't thought about the pace of my life here.

But you're right, I don't take breaks, often working seven days a week. It's something to consider."

"Maybe offer baked goods on certain days. Take a couple of days for yourself to do whatever you want."

"Is this coming from the police officer who works double shifts and steps in whenever there's a crime?"

She pulled open the door. "Pot. Kettle. Black. Yes, I'm guilty. Perhaps we should consider making changes in our lives. Marty's untimely death should be a reminder that we don't have a guaranteed long-term future. Those are my parting words of wisdom."

I laughed. "Night, Casey, drive carefully."

She jogged to her small pickup truck and climbed inside. The engine puttered to life. I waited until her headlamps swept the driveway before turning off the light. A sudden flash of a narrow beam of light made me freeze. Was someone on the other side of the fence hiding in the bushes?

"Hank, are you ready to go outside?" We'd go out the sliding door into the fenced-in yard. Just in case, I tucked pepper spray in my pocket for peace of mind. Animals didn't carry pen lights.

His nails clicked against the wooden floor as I snapped on the harness; he gave me the puppy side-eye as if to say, *Hey, we don't use a leash in my yard.* He wouldn't mind much if I gave him plenty of time to sniff.

The fenced-in space was awash in four flood lights, one on each corner of the lot. I scanned the yard while I carried him down the back steps onto the ground and let the leash out so he could do his thing.

The night was still except for Hank's snorts. I heard my cell ring inside the house. Why had I come outside without it? Whoever was calling would have to leave a message.

Hank froze and stared at the far corner of the fence line closest to the driveway. A low, deep growl made him sound as if he was the size of a wolf. The hair on his upper back spiked, but he didn't move.

I scooped him up. Holding him close to my chest, I murmured soothing words as I walked inside, closed and locked the door, and dialed 9-1-1. I hoped I wasn't being paranoid, but Hank rarely acted like this, and when he did, it was for a good reason.

I glanced at my text messages and saw one from an unknown number. As I read it, my blood chilled. It was straight out of a movie.

Stop meddling, or your little dog will end up alone, in a shelter.

I held him tighter and gazed out the window above the kitchen sink. A flicker of yellow and orange brightened the corner as flames licked the fence's slats. Right where Hank had growled. *FIRE!*

Without hesitation, I tapped the three digits and waited to be connected.

A calm male voice said, "9-1-1. What's your emergency?"

"This is Temperance Matthews. There's a fire at the back corner of my property. Two twenty-one Mahogany Street. Hurry."

The sounds of keys tapping came through the line. "Trucks are being dispatched. Are you in danger?"

"No, but my garage is." In the distance, I heard the tones of the fire trucks pierce the night. Help was on the way.

"Ms. Matthews, the fire department will arrive shortly. If you feel safe, please wait on the sidewalk until they arrive. Just stay out of the street."

"Thank you." I shoved the phone into my pocket and carried Hank through the house and out the front door. My hand hovered over the doorknob. "My car's in the driveway."

I ran back for the key, grabbed the fob from the hook, and raced out the back door. The car paint reflected the fire; the wooden stockade fence separating my land from the nature preserve was dry and the perfect fuel. I jumped in, placed Hank on the passenger seat, and threw the car in reverse as soon as the engine engaged. Moving the car would give the emergency crew better access and keep my fur baby safe.

Once on the street, I locked Hank in the car, raced to the barn-style garage doors, and flung them wide. The old-fashioned flower cart with metal wheels was against the back wall. I couldn't lose that on top of everything else. I had to save it!

The whine of the fire trucks reached me as I reached the back of the building. It and the cart were intact. Smoke curled under the wall. I raced forward, grabbed the cart handle and groaned. It wouldn't budge. Racing to the opposite side, I shoved with all my might. It moved! Not much, but it moved. I did that several more times before Erik Wool ran inside.

"Temperance, you have to get out of here. This whole place could become an inferno."

"Not. Without. This." I shoved again, and this time it moved two feet. The metal wheels needed grease.

Smoke seeped through the cracks in the walls. Choking on the smoke, I said, "Erik, help me. I lost my bakery; I can't lose this too."

He didn't hesitate. Together, we pushed it out the door. It glided down the short driveway, coming to a stop at a hose draped across the asphalt.

"Temperance, wait across the street. We've got this under control."

Turning away, I exhaled shakily. Stumbling to the car, I opened the passenger door and pulled Hank close to my chest. "It's going to be okay, little boy." I kissed his head and watched water stream from the hose being handled by two men. Smoke plumes rose, obscuring the stars. Would they be able to save my home and garage? In full turnout gear, members of the fire department rushed past me, dragging additional hoses, spraying down the flames, garage and the back of my home.

Sergeant Franklin strode in my direction, his face grim. "Temperance, what happened?"

"I don't know. When Casey was leaving, I noticed a narrow flashlight on the other side of the fence. I was concerned, but I didn't panic. When I took Hank out to go potty, he growled at that corner." I shifted him in my arms and removed my cell from my pocket. I handed it to him with the text message displayed. "I got this, and right after I read it, I saw the flames."

He glanced at the screen and returned the phone to me. "Do you recognize the number?"

I shook my head. "Who is doing this to me? Casey and I decided I was caught in the crosshairs of something involving the bakery, but now it seems..."

"Or you've annoyed the perpetrator by getting too close to the truth, and this a warning. The message infers you, not your dog, might be harmed."

The hair on the back of my neck prickled, and I was glued to the grass strip. "I don't know anymore."

"If anyone has been watching you, they know you've spoken with Louise, visited Jonah at the hospital, and talked with the police frequently."

"That's normal for a situation like this. The fire destroyed my business, my employees lost their jobs, and my friend, who sold me the building, was attacked. Of course, I'm on the outskirts of this case, and for the record, very few people know my background. I'd like to keep it that way."

"More people than you realize know where you worked. It's a small town and people love to talk."

"For Pete's sake, I could have been the receptionist or the guard at the entrance to the grounds."

His eyes bore into mine. "But we both know you weren't,

and the insight you've provided to Officer Butler is focusing our investigation."

I watched the fire department crew knocked back by the fire. Minutes felt like hours, yet they extinguished it quickly. They managed to save the house and garage by drenching it with water. The fence wasn't as lucky.

"Do you think there'll be evidence of who started this fire?"

"We'll find it," his voice oozed confidence. "I know this is a lot to handle—two fires in three days. I guarantee we will arrest this person."

"I've become the target."

"Would you like me to call Casey Butler? She can stay with you tonight. It might be a good idea if this firebug makes a return visit."

I didn't want to impose on our budding friendship. "That's okay. She's exhausted and needs her rest. Staying here, she won't get any."

He chuckled softly. "I might be her superior, but if I don't call her, she'll have some choice words for me. That's one cop who's in your corner until the end."

"I could call Josie if I got nervous."

"True, but Casey might be more of a deterrent."

"I know if I was on the wrong side of the match, she'd make me think twice before striking another one."

He smiled for the first time since he arrived. "Truth. So, you're okay if I give her a ring?"

"Perhaps text. This way, we won't disturb her if she's sleeping."

He narrowed his eyes. "Are you sure?"

"Yes."

Erik held his hand up to catch my attention and jogged over. "Good news. A few scorch marks on the back of the garage, but it doesn't look structural. You should have Russ Patterson inspect it when he's here next."

"You know he's doing work for me?"

Erik grinned, "Small towns, Temperance. But that's another conversation. We determined the source of the fire, and it was deliberate. It could have been bad if we hadn't had all the rain a few nights ago. The woods, along with your home and garage, might have been in danger."

Hank rested his head under my chin and snuggled close. I stroked his long back.

"Thank you for responding so fast and for your help with the cart. I realize it was foolish to go into the garage, but I couldn't bear losing more of my business to this madness. It looks like I need to drop off two batches of goodies at the firehouse."

"You don't. Our job is to protect and serve. However, if there is a next time, think twice before running into a building that's smoking."

Sergeant Franklin stepped away to answer his phone. I guessed it was Casey.

"Good safety tip." I didn't intend to sound as if I were making light of what I had done. It wasn't something I planned to do again.

"Temperance, Casey said she'd be here in ten minutes."

"I should call Josie so she doesn't hear about it and worry."

Erik bobbed his head to the fire truck. "We've got more work to finish, but I didn't want you to be concerned. If you'd like to go inside, the house is safe. I had two guys make a thorough inspection."

A lump lodged in my throat as I swallowed unshed tears.

Sergeant Franklin said, "Temperance, go inside. I'll make sure a patrol drives by a few times during the night. Just in case."

"Thank you. I know I keep saying it, but never has anything like this happened to me."

I carried Hank to the front door and went in, leaving the

lights off. I curled up on the sofa and dialed Josie. When she answered, the first thing I said was, "I'm okay."

"Temperance, what's happened?"

I gave her the full rundown of tonight's events, and she said, "I'm coming over."

"No. We're fine. Casey's coming over as an unofficial police presence. Tomorrow, we can fix everything. Fingers crossed, they'll be able to discover how the fire started."

"Are you sure? I can be there in minutes."

I heard the worry-laced words and appreciated her. "Come for coffee in the morning if you want."

"That's a given." She laughed softly to ease the tension. "I'm serious; if you need me any time during the night, please call. I'm placing my shoes and coat next to my car keys."

"You're a good friend, Josie. Thanks." I said goodnight and dropped the cell phone on the sofa.

All that remained was to wait for Casey. I needed to clear my head and reflect. *What am I overlooking?*

17

———

A sharp rap on the door followed by its opening. Hank's body tensed, and a low grumble vibrated deep in his chest.

Casey called out, "Temperance, where are you?"

"Living room." I ran a hand down Hank's spine to soothe him.

Casey rounded the corner, dropped a small tote bag on the floor, flicked on a table lamp, with a grim twist of her lips. "Did you want to have some excitement after I left?"

I offered her a tight smile to alleviate the oppressive atmosphere of the house. "Not really."

She removed her shoes and sank onto the couch, curling her feet underneath her. "Tell me what happened."

"I'm still not sure. After you backed out of the driveway, I noticed a small beam of light on the other side of the fence. It unnerved me a little, but I didn't want to think it was anything more than someone out for a late-night stroll on the walking path. It's happened before. Even though I was uneasy, I chalked it up to stress from the last few days. When I took Hank out for his potty break, I kept him leashed, and he growled while fixated on that corner. I brought him inside and stood at the kitchen window when I saw the fire. The dryness of the woods and the age of the fence, even after the rain, frightened me. I worried the fire would spread rapidly. I called the emergency number and backed my car to the street. Leaving my baby locked inside, I entered the garage to get the flower cart."

Her mouth gaped open at my statement of fact. "You ran into a burning building?"

"There weren't actual flames, yet. Just smoke. Remember, I had lost my bakery, and phase two was the flower cart. I had to get it out."

"I saw it on the driveway. You succeeded, but that was risky."

"When Erik Wool arrived, he found me struggling. Together, we managed to save it."

"You were lucky; the garage could have caught fire like dry paper."

I shuddered as my body trembled. The enormity of the night's events washed over me.

Casey slid over and put her arm around my shoulder. "It's over. You and Hank are safe."

I handed her my phone. "You need to see this."

She read out loud, "Stop meddling, or your little dog will end up alone in a shelter." She scratched Hank's ears, her eyes grave. "What the heck. That's a direct threat to you and your home."

"They imply either I won't have a home or Hank will be an orphan pup, but I won't back down."

"Did you tell Sarge about this?"

"Yes, that's why he insisted on calling you. Casey," my chin hit my chest, "I'm making someone nervous but to threaten Hank?" Tears slid over my face.

"It's okay. Let it out. You've had tremendous stress over the last two days. You realize the threat puts a completely different perspective on both fires."

Lifting my eyes to hers, I wiped my face and said, "I don't have the energy to talk about this. Can we change the subject?"

She nodded. "I'm going to check in with Sarge. I'll be right back."

"Of course, no problem." Hank buried his head in my sweatshirt and snuggled. We needed to draw comfort from one another. Closing my eyes, all I could see were flames licking up the fence. My cheeks grew damp again, and my pup licked my chin.

"We're going to be just fine, little boy. Tomorrow, the police will figure out what happened, and they'll know who to arrest so we can get started on the apartment demo."

Picking up the pad and pen from the table, I shifted on the sofa, stretching my legs out. *Making a list will clarify plans for the new venture.* I wrote—*dumpsters, donations, formal estimates, new equipment, small and large items, and baking supplies.* I tapped the pen against my leg. What should be on the menu? Start simple: *bread, chocolate chip cookies, corn muffins, and brownies.*

Satisfied with my progress, I made a list of ingredients for Peter. I wasn't ready for a delivery, but planning relaxed me. I sat up. "Wait a minute, the fire. Marty didn't start it; whoever lit the blaze tonight is the real arsonist."

Casey hurried in. "Did you say something?"

"Do you realize that tonight's fire proves perp two torched the bakery to cover up Marty's death? He might have gone there to create mischief or to stop it." My hand flew to cover my mouth. "Louise. We need to find out where she was tonight."

"That's already in the works." She frowned.

"Not good news?"

"We can't locate our four suspects, which means everyone remains on the list until we can obtain alibis, which we hope will happen by tomorrow."

"Does this mean we should hope for a sloppy arsonist?"

She gave me a half smile. "That's one way to look at it." Sitting beside me, she said, "The Sarge will send a patrol car by every hour until shift change at eight. Then, officers will swarm around your backyard and in the nature preserve like ants at a picnic. You don't need to worry; this was a huge mistake on the perp's part. We're close to an arrest. I can feel it in my bones."

"I wish I could connect the dots and find the pattern." I shook my head as the words rushed out. My brain raced as I finger-combed tangles from the length of my hair.

"Do you want to talk through the case and what we know now or wait until the morning? It might jog something for either of us. I don't know the suspects personally."

With a snort, I said, "I don't know anyone other than Jonah and Celeste, whom I met when I bought the bakery from them. I hired Gina and Louise. Peter is a vendor, and I met Alice, who came as a guest of Marty and Louise, to my party. The only people I'm friends with in town are Josie and Erik. And now you."

"Alice and Peter came to your party but were invited by Louise and Gina?"

With a nod, I said, "They mentioned a friend lived in town and didn't really know anyone. They thought Alice would be a fun addition. I said, sure, you know, the more the merrier. However, I was surprised she arrived as Peter's date."

"That doesn't align with what I've discovered. Alice moved to Oak Hollow over a year ago, moving from Atlanta, and she's been in a relationship with Peter for at least nine months."

"Huh. That's not long after the others arrived. But I don't remember seeing Alice until recently. She began coming into the bakery for day-old items, apparently for the children's afterschool program. On the day of the fire, Louise and Alice argued about the older baked goods. Wouldn't she have known why Alice wanted the day-old items if they were already friends?"

"That's a logical conclusion. Isn't it strange they'd ask to bring Peter and Alice to the party? Hasn't he been your delivery guy for a long time?"

"Since I opened."

"Then why would they ask to bring them to your event?"

"Now that you ask it like that, it seems odd. But more people milling around would make it easier to steal the key. If need be, someone could distract me or Josie."

Her brow furrowed.

I thought back to the party. "Everyone seemed to have a good time. Although I didn't witness a disagreement between Marty and Louise, they could have argued. I wouldn't have known about it at the time. It wasn't until I looked at the pictures that I realized there had been a heated exchange between Marty and Alice."

"Do you think it was about the key?"

"I don't. I thought Alice passed it to Louise. She definitely gave her something."

"Could Alice and Marty have been working together to frame Louise?"

"For what purpose?"

Casey stared out the window at the street. The quiet street and her thoughtful expression didn't alarm me.

"What if Louise planned to be fired? We know she wants to take an extended trip across the country. She could have convinced Marty to sneak into the bakery, commit petty vandalism, and have the evidence point in her direction. You find out, fire her, and she performs community service to atone for the crime. First-time offenders often receive a modest fine or a service requirement. It would be on her record, but maybe she didn't care."

"I don't know. It seems far-fetched. She could have quit, which is what Marty allegedly wanted her to do. Remember,

Gina and Louise want to take a road trip." I felt the color drain from my face. "They could be in on the plot together. Damage the bakery to shut me down, leaving them to collect unemployment and take a vacation." I placed Hank on the rug and paced the living room length three times before taking a deep breath. "What could Louise have been thinking? That it's okay to destroy someone's dream?"

"Good people do stupid things when they have tunnel vision."

"Why would Alice help them? She has nothing to gain and would lose a food source for her program. This is unbelievable." I continued to pace. "Marty agreed to help them. Did he want his girlfriend to run off with a friend? I'm missing something," I said, shaking my head. "Why would Alice attack Jonah?"

Casey's voice was steady. "There's no reason unless he heard or noticed something."

"I wish his memory would return." I whirled around and narrowed my eyes. "You don't think it was Louise, do you?"

Her voice remained steady. "No. If Louise, who fought with Marty inside the bakery, was the mastermind behind the vandalism, then she left the man she claims to love inside a burning building."

"Do you think Marty was the one who turned off the gas main?"

She nodded. "We believe it was him. Those shut-off valves are difficult to turn, even with the right tool. She panicked, added the oils and lit the fire."

"Are you suggesting this was just a case of vandalism that got out of hand?" I sank into an armchair while Hank curled up beside my feet.

"I do, and tomorrow, when it's daylight, I'm going to scour the burned area in the back and see if we can find any new clues pointing to her guilt."

"One thing escapes me: Louise never flinched when you

told her he had died, nor has she asked about her cat, while Gina had a small reaction. You really think that's normal?"

"If she were innocent, it could have been a shock. Gina's response was typical as a friend."

"If Louise had already known Marty was dead, she could have exaggerated her response like what you see in the movies."

"That would be a reasonable assumption."

"Can I ask about the screenshots you took of Gina's phone, or is that confidential information?"

"Can it be off the record?"

I nodded. "You wouldn't have done that if something hadn't piqued your interest."

"After her fight with Marty, Louise was distraught and left the house at nine. She said she called Gina soon after leaving, but Louise said Gina didn't answer. After driving around, she parked the car at eleven before going for a walk. However, she texted Marty before nine. If she had been home, why send a text? There was a text to Gina that said, *hey*. If there was a text conversation between Gina and Louise, it was deleted, and I only saw one missed call. Why did Louise lie and Gina cover for her?"

"Why haven't you brought her in yet?"

"We're still gathering information, and after you mentioned that they were considering leaving town and using unemployment for income, we've been monitoring their movements. So far, they haven't filed a claim."

"They could have completed the process online."

Casey gave me a confident smile. "Not in our state."

"That's interesting." I slumped against the cushions. "There's still something I'm missing, and I can't put my finger on it."

"I have a question for you. You mentioned Louise and Gina's keys only opened the front door. Is it possible they thought the color coding was random?"

"I never explicitly told them that the masters are pink, and theirs were purple."

"Would you say the colors would appear similar if placed side by side, considering a person is color blind?"

I felt the smile grow on my face. "What if Marty couldn't tell the difference between pink and purple since there are many variations to colorblindness."

She nodded. "It's not a stretch to say that he wouldn't realize he had the wrong key."

"And Marty wouldn't know the ladies only had front door keys."

"That's right, since most employees could have a key that opens front and back."

"Casey, can we confirm he was colorblind? Is it noted on his driver's license? Oh, wait, just a minute." I snapped my fingers. "Louise mentioned it when we were on the porch after I complimented the color of the flower pots. She said he was supposed to buy yellow and pink not purple."

18

———

With a mug of steaming coffee in my right hand, I hunched over my laptop when Casey strode through the back door. I jerked in the chair and clutched my chest, willing my heart to return to a normal rhythm. "When did you go outside?"

"An hour ago, I heard you stirring and figured you'd be in the kitchen soon. I wanted to check out the scene behind the house."

"Did you find anything?"

"Two officers have secured and cordoned off the area, but they discovered a lighter and a stack of newspapers that hadn't ignited. They were this week's edition of The OH Gazette." She filled a mug by the pot and pulled out a chair.

Hank lifted his head, looked at Casey and then me, and promptly lay back down to continue his first nap of the day.

Someone brought the papers there. "Why would someone want to hurt me?"

"I don't think they do. They used the fire last night, just like the bakery, as a tool; the text and fire are meant to frighten you into abandoning the case."

"Who knows I'm doing anything other than cooperating with an investigation for a crime against me?"

Sipping her coffee, she set her mug on the table. "Anyone who knows your previous profession understands that people like us—defenders of what's right and wrong—don't stop living by our ethics and morals, even if we change jobs. It's part of our DNA, just like our eye color or height."

Sitting tall, I asked, "Why are you so nice to me? When we met two days ago, it felt as if you could barely tolerate me."

For the first time since Casey walked into the room, she smiled, one that warmed her eyes. "From the first time I asked you questions, I saw myself in you. The way you scanned the crowd, processed information, and included me in your findings was impressive. All you wanted was justice to be served, not just for you, but for Marty."

"Why wouldn't I?'

"People with your background aren't known to share intel with local police."

"Those are field agents, not analysts. It's our responsibility to be transparent with all the information we uncover."

"From a small-town cop's perspective, you've been extremely helpful. The concern you've shown to everyone is genuine. The only person having an issue is the guilty one."

The oven timer dinged. I stood, "I hope you like carrot muffins."

"If I don't have to bake, I'm always a willing participant in the eating process," she grinned. "I can whip up some eggs if you like. That's one thing I'm great at, scrambled only though."

My stomach grumbled. "Sounds good. What time do you need to take off?"

"After breakfast. I'm going to work at four, but I want to check in at the station to see if there's any other information about either fire."

I took the tray of muffins out of the oven and set them on

the counter. "I've been thinking about last night. You mentioned our suspects weren't home."

"I received that update. Apparently, it was a girl's night out. Gina, Louise, and Alice said they went to the movies to help take their mind off everything that has happened."

Crossing my arms over my stomach, I leaned against the counter. "Which film did they see?"

"That's the detail I'm missing, and of course, we'll go to the theater later to see if anyone can verify they were there. Producing a ticket stub isn't confirmation they were in the building."

"Even if they did go, there's no way to know they stayed for the entire movie. One of them could have slipped out, come over here, started the first, and sent the text."

She nodded. "It's a disposable phone with no way to trace it."

"Figures, and Peter?"

"We can verify he was restocking his truck for deliveries today."

I sighed and flipped the muffin tray over, and once they were on the rack, I filled a plate.

"Temperance, I understand this is frustrating; we will apprehend the responsible party. You have my word."

"Before they come at me again or attack another innocent person like Jonah?"

"We're doing our best." Her words stung like an angry hornet.

"In my previous job, it wasn't personal; it was data to analyze and use to inform the agents on the front line. Being in the loop, well, not really, but closer than I have been is difficult, and I'm the target."

A tap on the back door caught my attention. Russ waved at me.

I walked across the room and held the door. "Come in. Casey and I are having breakfast. Would you like to join us?"

"Coffee would hit the spot." He glanced over his shoulder, where he had a clear view of the garage. "I heard about the trouble last night. Would you like me to check the garage's structural integrity to see if it's safe or needs repairs?"

"Sure. The firemen did a great job keeping the flames at bay, but it wouldn't hurt." I noticed the large manila envelope in his hand. "Is that the estimate for the new kitchen?"

"It sure is, and don't worry. It's not bad. The apartment's bones are excellent, and I've estimated an on-demand water heater to handle the high temperatures you need for sanitizing. I included air conditioning since summer can be brutal in a kitchen, and ceiling fans aren't permitted per health department codes."

"Did you figure in my doing some work too?" I pulled out a chair for him.

He sat down, and I handed him a mug of steaming coffee. Casey gave him a small plate with a muffin. I appreciated how she had made herself comfortable.

"You can do as much or as little as you like. I've included a column showing the amounts you can save by pitching in, and you can decide where you want to save or spend."

"What a clever idea. I'll look at it later. Where can I rent a dumpster for the debris?"

"I'll order that for you. Just say the word, and it should be delivered in a couple of days."

"I'll apply for the permit today. As soon as I have that in hand, we can start."

He nodded. "You know, I went by the bakery this morning."

Casey looked at me and stepped closer to the table. "Oh?"

"The yellow tape is gone. Does that mean we should plan for a crew to come in and begin clearing the site?"

Her brow furrowed. "Let me check into that. I didn't know the investigation was complete, and given what happened here last night, I'd be surprised if it was released."

She picked up her cell from the counter and walked from the room.

Russ toyed with his mug. "I hope there's nothing wrong at the site."

I refilled my cup and sat. "Everything that's happened over the last few days has been awful." I shook my head and sipped my coffee. My pulse jittered. Intent to talk about something other than the fires, I asked, "How long will it take to renovate the apartment into a working kitchen?"

He grinned. "There's a bright spot in the morning. My crew is happy to work part of Saturday to help speed up the process. People are already missing your bakery, myself included. Once you have the permit, I have volunteers ready to move all the furniture into the garage, well, once I ensure it's stable. If it's not, I can lend you a storage building until you figure out what you're keeping and how you want to dispose of the rest."

Wiping away the tears from my eyes, I said, "People have volunteered to move the furniture?"

He nodded, "And help with the demolition. You don't realize it, Temperance, but many people in town think highly of you, and they know what happened wasn't your fault. They want to help."

"I'm speechless."

He laughed softly. "You're going to need to find your voice to direct the helpers when we start moving things."

The sincerity in his deep brown eyes shifted something deep inside me. The corners of my mouth turned up. "I'm sure that won't be a problem. Are you thinking we'll do this in two days, empty the apartment, and then folks will come back and help with the demo?"

"From what I saw yesterday, moving the furniture shouldn't take more than a couple hours. The demo will take an entire day. What do you think if I get a dumpster here as soon as they can deliver?"

"Sounds good to me."

He nodded toward the adjoining door. "We'll need to seal that entrance to minimize dust seeping through the cracks in the door into your home."

"Today, I'll make a list of items I want to keep. The bedroom will become the office, so that will be a clean sweep, and the stuff in good condition will be donated."

"If you want a curb-free sale, we can put the furniture and dishes outside and post it on social media. That way, people can take what they want."

"Then we wouldn't have to haul it anywhere." I nodded. "That sounds like a good idea."

Casey walked in, and the frown on her face caused my stomach to drop. "Someone removed the tape during the night. When the cruiser went down the street at one, it was there; by three, it was gone, and no one was around."

I pressed my fingers to my temples to ward off the headache that was building. "Why? There's nothing valuable there."

"Someone thinks differently," she said, crossing the kitchen to the stove. "Eggs?"

Russ stood, "I'm going to take off via the garage. Call when you have the permit, and I'll handle the dumpster and volunteers."

"Casey, I'll be back in a few minutes. I'm going with Russ to assess the fire damage."

She nodded, lost in thought. If I could see inside her mind, I'd expect to see wheels turning.

Russ held the door, and I stepped outside. The air carried a faint, acrid smell of smoke. At first glance, my shoulders sagged, looking at what remained of the charred fence, which was an easy fix. The front of the garage had streaks of smoke residue, but nothing that a power wash couldn't remedy.

"So far, it doesn't look too bad." We walked to the right of the building and down the narrow path to the back. This was the first time I saw the scorched earth and back of the building.

Running his hand over the smoky siding, he smiled. "Good news. The cedar is solid. A fresh coat of paint, and it'll look like new."

"That's the best news I've had so far." I picked my way to where the fence was gone and squatted down. I studied it from one angle and then another. "Well, well."

"Did you find something?"

I looked at him and smiled. "Yes." I wanted to pick it up but held back. "Casey needs to see this." I sent a quick text asking her to join us.

As Russ and I walked further down the fence line, I paused with every step, curious whether anything else could help identify the firebug.

"Do you need me to bring a few stockade panels to fix this?"

"No, thanks, you've got enough of my projects to manage. I'll call the fence company I used, and they can make the repairs. However, I'll have to wait for the insurance people again. It feels like I'm in a hurry-up-and-wait mode."

I heard the screen door bang and footsteps approaching the fence line.

"Temperance?"

"Come around the garage."

Casey stepped over what was left of the fence. "This is faster. Did you find any evidence?"

I pointed to where the fire originated, or I guessed it had since there was the most damage. "It could be a clue to the identity of our not-so-friendly fire enthusiast." I was tired of using the word *arson*.

"You didn't touch anything, did you?"

"Nope. I have walked the fence line to see what else might have been left behind, but I didn't see anything else."

"Show me what you uncovered here."

Russ stepped back to give us plenty of room.

"Look. Isn't that part of a medical ID bracelet?"

"I wonder how that got overlooked," she said.

"If the sun hadn't caught it just right I would have missed it."

She pulled out her phone and took pictures from every angle. "I don't have an evidence bag, so we'll need to wait until the officers arrive, but good work." She gave me a thumbs up. "Another piece of the puzzle."

"People with diabetes wear medical ID bracelets."

"True, but until we examine it, we won't know what medical concern is listed, assuming the fire didn't destroy the information."

Here I was, excited I might have found an important clue to cement Louise's guilt, only to realize maybe it wouldn't.

Casey glanced at the ground and picked up a small stick. Squatting down, she carefully turned over the bracelet and leaned closer. "Asthma. The rest of the information has been scratched off."

I peered over her shoulder. "Do you think it was intentional?"

"It's hard to say. If someone has worn this for a long time, it may simply be wear and tear, depending on their job."

She tossed the stick aside and stood. "We need to keep this information between the three of us. I can't let anyone else know." Her gaze was fixed on Russ.

He raised his hands. "I didn't see anything. I was here to discuss construction. Nothing more."

With a brisk nod, she said, "I'll wait for the officers to collect this new evidence. You two should head back to the house."

"Should I stay?" Russ asked.

Casey was focused on the scorched ground. "There's no need, but if I have questions, I'll call you."

"Anytime. Happy to help."

We walked around the garage, my eyes glued to the ground in case we missed something else. However, there wasn't much to see except lots of boot prints from the firefighters tramping the ground. Once in the driveway, I halted.

Russ asked, "What's wrong?"

"I've got company." I noticed the newcomers' blank stares directed at my house; our gazes locked.

He followed mine to the middle of the street. "What are they doing here?"

"That's an excellent question."

"You're not expecting them?"

"They've been here more often since the fire than they have been in the last eighteen months."

He brushed my hand with his, and under his breath he said, "I'm not going anywhere."

19

———————

*G*ina and Louise rushed forward. "Temperance, we heard about the fire last night and came over to see how you are." They wrapped their arms around me with a hug, pushing Russ aside. "Are you all right?"

I pulled back; if they had heard about the fire last night, why didn't they reach out? "Hank and I are both fine. We're a little stressed, but nothing more serious than replacing a few panels on the fence, and Russ confirmed the garage is sturdy."

Alice smiled at him. "That's the best news we've had today."

"How *did* you hear?"

Gina said, "Alice called, and we had to come over to check on you. This is not your week."

"I'm sure it'll get better. Would you like to come in for coffee? Russ and I were going into the kitchen."

"That's okay. Now that we know you're safe, we'll head home," Louise looked at the ground and then at me. "We've decided to take a trip while you're rebuilding. Then, when we get back, maybe you'll be ready for us to work."

"The bakery won't reopen for well over a year." I wasn't

sure why I said that since Russ hadn't given me a projected timeline yet.

Gina glanced at the flower cart in my front yard. "I thought you were opening a mobile bakery. Won't you need help?"

"That will also take time; initially, it will be on a small scale."

Her face paled. "Are you firing us?"

The hostile tone in her voice set off a warning bell in my head. "Of course not. I've been thrilled with your work. The fire was beyond my control, and my best chance to maintain people's interest in purchasing my baked goods, is the little bakery. After I renovate the apartment in the house, it'll be a small operation."

Russ said, "There isn't much space in the new area."

I placed my hand on his arm, appreciating his support. "If I could bring you both on, I would. I can keep you updated on the reconstruction during your travels. Once the new building is complete, a job will be waiting if you want it. Until then, collecting unemployment will maintain your cash flow, and you can take some time to decompress."

Louise remained silent, almost as if she didn't care whether she got her job back. Perhaps Marty's desire for her to quit reflected her own desire to move on.

"You don't care if we take off for a few months?" Louise asked.

"Why not make the most of this time?" The words tasted like sawdust in my mouth as I stood in front of an arsonist and killer.

She said, "Gina, we should leave. Temperance has things to do, and we need to plan our next steps."

Gina looked between us, her brow furrowed as if she felt the unexplained tension. "If you need anything, give us a call, and we'll let you know when we plan to leave town."

"Don't forget, you must sign up for your unemployment

benefits in person." I wasn't sure why I said that, but it made me feel as though I was trying to help them in a small way.

"We appreciate the information," Louise said.

They turned to leave, and I asked, "Where did you park?"

Gina said, "We walked over. It was good to clear the fog. The last few days have strained Louise, and her glucose numbers haven't been stable. Exercise is good for both of us."

With a nod, Louise said, "Stress can do that. Last night, I went to bed early because I felt unwell."

"Are you better today?" I looked to see if there was a difference in her demeanor.

"Much. Thanks. Catch you later."

I waited until they reached the corner before calling out to Casey. I grabbed Russ's arm. "That's something she needs to know."

He said, "I'm going to take off, but we'll talk later."

"You bet. Thanks for everything."

I waited until he had backed out of the driveway before jogging around the garage and meeting Casey halfway. "I had visitors."

"Oh? Who?"

"Gina and Louise. Guess what they just shared?"

"I'm terrible at games; just tell me."

"In the last few days, Louise hasn't been feeling well; the stress is wreaking havoc on her blood sugar, so she went to bed early last night."

She lifted a single eyebrow and cocked her head. "What did you say?"

"I asked if she was feeling better, and she said yes."

"Did Gina react to her comment?"

"Not even a flinch. Either Louise has proof that she was in bed early, or Gina doesn't realize that admitting going to bed early could imply Louise's guilt. And get this, Gina said Alice called them about the fire last night."

"Good work. I will check into their alibis, starting with the phone call from Alice."

A cruiser pulled up to the service road in the nature preserve. "You've got company, and I'm heading back to the kitchen to finish making breakfast. All this drain of brainpower is making me hungry."

She laughed. "Save some for me." Before walking away, she added, "Have you heard from Celeste and Jonah today?"

"Not yet; I plan to call around ten. She might need help getting him settled at their place if he's getting discharged. Why?"

"I'm curious if his memory is back."

"If she says anything, I'll let you know."

Once I was in the house, fully caffeinated and alone, I decided to call Celeste, but it went to voicemail, so I left her a message.

"Hi, Celeste and Jonah. I just wanted to check in and see how things are going today. Please call me when you get the chance."

I tidied the kitchen while Hank danced around my feet. "Do you want to go for a walk?" I snapped his harness on. As an afterthought I texted Casey to let her know we were going around the block.

With his nose to the pavement, he took the lead in the opposite direction from Josie's. We'd go past her house on the way home. We stopped every minute or so to do another sniffer sweep. Not that I minded; the morning was picture perfect, warm enough so I didn't need a jacket with the sun in a bright blue sky, the light breeze teasing my ponytail.

The mulch-covered walkway leading into the nature preserve was irresistible to Hank. With his tail wagging, we strolled down the path, one of his favorite places to walk. Gina and Louise were ahead, sitting on the bench near the pond. It was possible this was the exact spot where she had come after her argument with Marty.

My steps slowed as I grew closer. What was that in Gina's hand? An inhaler. How could I have forgotten she had asthma? My stomach clenched, but the nerves jangling didn't deter me.

"Hi, ladies. I didn't realize you were coming to the park."

Gina dropped her hand to her lap. Louise looked up, her eyes rimmed with red. "I just couldn't handle running into any more people," she said. "Everyone saying how sorry they are about Marty. Not that I wished him dead, but he wasn't a saint."

"I can empathize with you. You've been through a lot. In people's defense, knowing what to say in this situation is difficult. It was awful to have died tragically." I hated to bait Louise like this, but I had so many questions and needed answers.

She nodded. "I get that too. I hope he didn't suffer."

Gina said, "He didn't." She stood and added, "Louise, we should get back to my place so we can stop by the unemployment office after lunch."

"Good luck." I wasn't sure what else to say as they left. Hank barked and wagged his tail. "I know, little one. Two clues just presented themselves. We need to talk to Casey as soon as we finish our loop. Those two aren't going anywhere. They need money to fund their escape." I scooped him up and carried him down the path.

When I reached the street near my former bakery, I discovered Celeste and Jonah's car parked near the hardware store. He was in the passenger seat, so I waved and jogged over.

"Hi, Jonah. Seeing you out of the hospital is a relief."

He pushed open the passenger door, got out, and gave me a bear hug. "You're okay."

"Of course."

He scanned the area and said, "We should sit on the bench." He dropped his voice. "I remember everything."

I placed Hank on the ground and slipped my arm through

Jonah's, guiding him to a bench. The front door faced us so we could see when Celeste came out. I wanted to ask him what he saw, but there was no point in rushing him. The memories needed to resurface without pressure in case there were still gaps.

Clasping his hands, he hung his head. "I should have told you weeks ago, but to be honest, at the time, I didn't think it was a big deal."

"Something happened at my party?" Setting the pup on the bench between me and Jonah, his head swiveled from side to side, nose twitching.

He nodded. "I was getting a fresh ketchup bottle; do you remember me asking you where it was?"

"Sure. I said I'd get it, but you offered to help since I was grilling."

"Right. When I walked in, Gina was putting a key into her pocket. I must have given her a strange look since she said she dropped her house key. At the time, I didn't think much of it, but later, I overheard Alice asking Gina if she got what she came for, and she replied yes, she got the pink one. That's when I remembered I had suggested you color code the front and back door keys. It was after Celeste had mixed them up when she handed them to you at the closing."

"The new colored keys made it easier to keep track of who had what." At least now I knew Alice didn't pass the key to Louise; however, she and Gina are very close. Maybe she palmed the key for Louise. "Have you told Officer Butler?"

"Not yet. We'll go to the station after Celeste picks up a few things."

"Good, you should." I stood, and he grabbed my arm.

"Wait."

I sat back down.

"I mentioned that Alice, Peter, and Erik were at Sassy's the night I was stabbed. I couldn't remember who else until late last night. Gina and Louise were there, having drinks but not at the table with the others. I assumed they were waiting for their pizza. Gina approached the counter to get another pale ale. Our eyes met, and that's when it clicked. I must have frowned since her cheeks changed from rosy to ghostly white. *She* had the key for Marty to gain access to the bakery the night it burned."

A hard knot tightened my gut. "It was Gina."

He swallowed hard. "Just before I felt the knife I smelled beer as the attacker closed in on me. I'm ninety-five percent certain it was Gina who stabbed me."

Nodding, I said, "Because she knew you were coming to tell me she stole the key from my house."

Tears welled up in his eyes. "I'm sorry, Temperance. None of this would have happened if I had told you what happened at your picnic."

His emotional outburst surprised me, and I believed it was more about being in the hospital after the attack than about not sharing that detail with me. "You need to tell the police everything you told me."

"I will."

Celeste raced across the street, holding a small brown paper bag. "Jonah, you should be in the car and not over-taxing yourself."

"I had to tell Temperance the whole truth."

"Aside from the brief walk from the car to the bench, we've been chatting." I wanted to reassure her I wasn't pressuring Jonah.

"Stubborn man." She kissed the top of his head. With eyes darting, she said, "Did he tell you everything?"

I dipped my chin. "Yes, I heard you're going to the station next."

A sharp glint appeared in Celeste's eyes. "We have to. That woman can't get away with hurting people."

It wasn't far-fetched to believe that Gina had set the fire behind my house last night. What had I ever done to her that made her want to destroy my business or scare me into silence? I stood, unsure what to do next, and squeezed Jonah's hand. "I'm glad you're feeling better."

"Me too, but now I'm worried about you. Stay vigilant. That woman is capable of anything."

Sad but true, I nodded in agreement. "Can I help you back to the car?"

He said, "Yes, please. This kerfuffle has taken more out of me than I thought." Rising to his feet, his gait unsteady, I placed my hand under his elbow. "Take your time. I've got all day." I smiled, hoping it would lessen his agitation. I slipped Hank's leash over my arm, and he walked beside us. It took several minutes for Jonah to cross the short distance. He was huffing when he leaned against the car. I opened the passenger door and gave him a moment before he got in.

"Temperance. I'm sorry, but we just did the senior shuffle. You've got better things to do than tend to an old man."

"No need to apologize for anything. Besides, you're hardly old, just recovering from an injury, and as I mentioned, I'm in no rush." Especially since I was uncertain what to do next. "Would you like me to accompany you and Celeste to the police station?"

He shook his head. "No, but if you'd like to let Officer Butler know we'll be there soon, that would be helpful."

"Consider it done." I took his arm and guided him into the car, waiting until he buckled his seatbelt before I shut the door.

"Being in pain stinks."

"Allow yourself time to heal. Before long, you'll be strolling through the town center with your finger on the pulse of everything."

"Goodbye, Temperance. After this is over and that woman is arrested, tell me your plans for rebuilding the bakery."

I laughed. "Always thinking about the future."

He chuckled. "Aren't you?"

Celeste had gotten into the car and started it. She leaned across Jonah and waved. "Bye, doll."

I waited until they pulled away from the curb before dialing Casey. Hank and I strode back to the bench with a view of my burnt-out store in front of me. The moment I heard her say hello, I spoke. "It's Gina. Jonah's on his way to the station to make a statement. I don't know why she did it, but I intend to find out."

"Temperance, slow down. What do you know?"

"Gina burned down my bakery, tried to cast suspicion onto Louise, stabbed Jonah, and I'm sure she started the fire at the fence, too, and she uses an inhaler for her asthma."

"How do you know that?"

"When I took Hank for a walk, we went by the pond. She and Louise were sitting on the bench, and she was using an inhaler. I remembered she had used it the night of the fire when she was worried about Louise being inside the bakery. Additionally, Louise expressed hope that Marty didn't feel any pain in the fire, and Gina confidently asserted that he didn't. She knew he was already dead." Hank gave a sharp bark, and I glanced across the street. My heart stilled.

"Do you know where Gina is now?"

"Yes. She's staring at me from in front of what's left of my bakery."

20

———

*C*asey's voice cracked like a whip through the phone line. "Do not engage Gina. Where are you?"

"Across the street from my bakery, but…" The line went dead before I could say, "I'm headed home."

I weighed my options. Should I stay in plain sight of a murderer or try to get away? Hank whined and nudged my arm. I didn't want my fur baby caught in the crossfire. "Come on, little boy, I'll take you to Josie's; you'll be safe with her. I need to deal with a cranky lady."

I texted Josie. *Stopping over with Hank. Can you keep him while I take care of something?*

A smiley emoji came back a second later.

I placed him on the ground, hoping to appear casual, and as much as I didn't want to turn my back on Gina, I had to. She had stabbed a kind man once; she could do it again. This time, I'd stay on the sidewalk or even walk in the middle of the road to draw attention to myself.

Moving at a brisk pace, reaching Josie's would take less than ten minutes. We walked down South Street and turned onto Vine Street. After living in a city for many years, I knew when I was being followed and was sure Gina was behind me, keeping a safe distance.

What was I going to say when I confronted her? Demand to know why she broke into my bakery and lit the match? What had I done to her? Why did she fight with Marty and then not even try to help him? Questions tumbled over and over.

Josie's house stood on the corner, a sanctuary for Hank, while my heart hammered in my chest. I was so close. I stubbed my sneaker on the uneven surface, catching myself as my knee hit the cement sidewalk. At least I avoided a face plant.

"Temperance, are you okay?" Gina jerked my arm as I sat up.

"Thanks, just a bit clumsy." I looked around; we were alone. Hank grumbled and nudged my hand. I brushed the pebbles off and gingerly rose to my feet, my knee already growing stiff.

"Are you going home?"

I couldn't tell her I was going to Josie's; putting her in the line of fire was out of the question. "Yes, I'm taking the long way. I'm giving Hank some much-needed exercise since I've been so busy since the fire."

"I'm sure it has been. That's why I've been trying to catch up to you. I wanted to discuss the fire."

My brow ratcheted to my hairline. "Oh? You should tell Officer Butler or Sergeant Franklin if you have new information. I believe they're close to making an arrest."

Her eyes flickered in surprise. "That's what I heard earlier today. A couple of officers were at the bakery, and I was eavesdropping. Did you know during the night someone took down the yellow crime scene tape? I wonder why. Do you suppose whoever did that was tired of the reminder of the fire?"

"So it would seem. There isn't any other reason to remove

it." I echoed her thoughts to see if it would spark another reaction. She smiled as she recognized what I had done.

"Do you have a theory? What someone might be looking for?" She crossed her arms over her chest and stared at me.

"A piece of jewelry, perhaps?" I let Hank's leash drop to the ground. He was well trained and wouldn't leave me unless I gave him a specific command, no matter what squirrel or bird crossed our path.

She nodded her approval. "You are quite intelligent and would be better suited to something other than baking bread."

"Been there, done that, and made a pivot." I stepped back, hoping it was so minor she wouldn't notice.

She grabbed my arm. "Not so fast."

"I'd like to get Hank home. Walking is thirsty for a little dog."

"Later. You're coming with me. We need to clarify a few details before I leave town with Louise."

I looked at her fingers digging into my forearm. "You should take your hand off me."

"Not likely. I'll say what I came to say, and you'll keep that mouth shut. If you don't, your little dog has drunk his last bowl of water."

I lifted my chin in defiance. "You have two minutes to speak before I make you limp to the police station."

She snorted. "Bravo, Temperance. But we both know you were a pencil pusher with the bureau. There's nothing you can do to me other than spew facts. So, listen up. Marty was not a nice guy. He was a terrible boyfriend, and all he ever wanted was for Louise to quit and get a better-paying job so he didn't have to work. That was the last straw for me when he decided to trash the bakery and make it look like she did it. When she called to say they'd had another fight, I went over there. I even brought the pale ale beer he likes."

"So you were the extra mug in the sink."

She grinned. "Details. Good for you. He bragged that he would make sure you fired Louise in the morning, and he had taken her bakery key. The idiot was color-blind and never realized there were two keys. It was just his luck he took the master which I," she titled her head from side to side, "borrowed from you and slipped onto her keyring."

"Why did you take it?"

"Why not? You never know when a master key might come in handy. But I'm getting off track. With Louise out of the house, I promised to meet him there to help."

"You wanted me to fire your friend?"

She scowled. "Of course not. I lied. I was going to make sure everyone knew Marty did it and that Louise was innocent. I lifted his work badge from the house and planned on planting it at the bakery for the police to find. That was until I walked in and saw he had dumped every powdered item on top of the paper mess he'd created. We argued, and he grabbed me. Then I shoved him. That's when he fell back and hit his head against the oven door. I panicked and left him there. When I walked outside, I had second thoughts, so I went back, dumped oil on the mess and dropped the lighter. I thought no one would discover what had really happened."

"And the hoodie?"

"A diversion. Louise has no idea I was involved, and she never will." She tightened her grip on my arm and jerked me forward.

"Hank! Josie's now!"

He hesitated and, with a low growl, barred his teeth at Gina. I shouted to him again, "Josie's now!"

This time, he did as I commanded and ran as fast as his little legs would move. I knew he'd make a beeline to the front door and bark to be let in.

Gina dragged me to the stand of trees across the street. I stumbled as my knee gave out. "I think my leg's broken."

"It's not far." Gina's blue eyes were still as frozen pond water.

I couldn't hear Hank barking anymore the farther she dragged me into the woods, and I hoped Josie would realize something was terribly wrong.

"You don't need to hurt me. We can forget about the fire, let the police bungle the investigation, and the insurance company will pay for all the damages."

She glared at me. "Right. Like you'd ever let me walk away. You hold Peter accountable for every piece of fruit he delivers to the bakery. If he tries to give you too much, you insist on paying for it. You're such a Goody Two-shoes. There's no way you'll let me off the hook."

"Maybe not, but you did all this because you were sticking up for Louise." Unsure how far we walked, we stopped in a small clearing. Lost in the preserve, I couldn't hear any traffic on Vine Street. The clearing isolated us. "Why didn't you encourage her to break up with the man?"

Rolling her eyes, she said, "You saw them at your picnic; she was besotted and believed the sun rose because it was his wish." She let go of my arm and withdrew a small handgun. "Before you think you can run, forget about it. A bullet moves faster than fire."

"Louise's talking like she's glad he's dead as if he had been an albatross around her neck."

"All to cover her grief. It's easier for her to cope, and I've tried to plant a few ideas in her head, but I can see why you'd get the wrong impression."

"Why did you set the fire last night and send the text threatening me?"

"You think that was me?"

"Gina, as you've said, I'm sharp," I locked eyes with her, "like the paring knife you used to stab Jonah. You took that from Sassy's."

"That. Yeah, I'm not happy I hurt Jonah—it was a weapon of opportunity. I've always liked him."

"Then why?"

She stamped her foot on the pine needle-covered ground, her breath becoming labored. "I needed time to get away. If you hadn't been asking questions, he might not have remembered that he saw me take the key from your house." She waved the gun. "Enough talking. We're done. You'll walk through the woods until we reach the pond."

"And then you plan to shoot me and toss me into it?"

With a shrug, she said, "Stop talking. You're confusing me."

It appeared she was muddled. Scanning the area, I saw that there weren't any branches on the ground I could use to knock the gun from her hand. But I needed for her to take a shot at something. The sound would alert Josie, combined with Hank's arrival without me she'd have called the police.

Patting her jeans pockets, she murmured, "Where is it?" Birds cawed in the trees, and she jumped at the sound of them taking flight. "I need my inhaler." She pointed to the path while keeping the gun directed at my chest. "Move."

"Should we go back and find it?" Could I appeal to her sense of self-preservation?

"No time. Move."

"There's plenty of time." Where were squirrels and other small animals that scampered through the woods when I needed the distraction? The birds weren't helping.

I heard a series of high-pitched barks. Hank. Gina swung around, training the gun in the direction of his barking. I rushed her, tackling her to the ground.

Twice, the gun went off. *BANG! BANG!*

I prayed the bullet didn't hit him.

I heard Hank. *Yip.*

Had he been shot? It took all my strength as I pressed

against the central veins running down her arm to her hand as I wrestled the weapon away. "Drop it now!"

"No." She squirmed to get out from under me. Her breath came in quick, ragged bursts. She slumped to the ground, her hand relaxed, and I tossed the weapon aside.

"Temperance!" Casey burst into the clearing, gun drawn, with Sergeant Franklin and another officer I didn't know.

Hank squirmed in Josie's arms, his high-pitched barks growing more agitated.

Casey helped me up. "What happened?"

I pointed to the discarded gun. "Gina confessed to everything. She was going to kill me and leave town. You might want to place her under arrest and then get the EMTs to transport her to the hospital. She's having an asthma attack and lost her inhaler."

My knees collapsed, and I sank to the ground. Josie placed Hank down, and he leaped into my arms, showering my face with kisses.

"It's okay, little boy. I'm fine, and you did a good job." I looked at Josie. "Thank you."

"The moment he showed up without you, I called Casey. By the time she arrived, you had disappeared into the thicket. We only knew where you were headed when Hank darted across the street.

"It felt like we walked for hours." I nuzzled him close and kissed his little black head. "You're a smart little baby."

"I watched Gina dragging you into the woods. I wanted to follow you, but I had to wait for Casey. She wanted me to stay in the house. Hank had other ideas."

Casey came over. "I know you had training that Josie didn't. It was a calculated risk."

"And it was the right call. If I had known Josie and Hank were following me, I couldn't have gotten Gina's confession."

"Well done." Casey bobbed her head toward Gina, who

was now handcuffed, sitting cross-legged on the ground. "Emergency will be here in a few minutes. You'll need to make a statement, but for now, head home, have some coffee, sit on your front porch, and watch the world go by." She glanced at my knee. "Do you need medical attention?"

"No, I pretended it was worse than it was to move slower."

Casey grinned. "Smart lady."

I nodded. "Louise didn't know. Gina tried to direct the clues to implicate her, believing she had an airtight alibi in all instances."

"Your help is appreciated. Josie, can you hang out with Temperance today?"

Then it hit me, I looked between the two women; I had two good friends. Smiling, I said, "The coffee pot will be on if you want to swing by."

THREE DAYS LATER, I secured Hank in my home office with his water, treats, extra blankets and bed, along with my favorite classic rock music playing. A large red, open-topped dumpster sat in my driveway, and ten people were moving various items from the apartment, including chairs, dressers, a bed, boxes of kitchen utensils, and a small metal kitchen table that dated back to the mid-century. Josie directed people at the end of the driveway and on the sidewalk, instructing them to line everything up for easy access during the curb-free sale.

Russ strolled over to me, wearing a yellow hard hat, and handed one to me. His brown eyes were like liquid chocolate this morning. Leave it to me to equate this man's eyes with food. But hey, what else would I do? I'm a baker.

"Are you ready to start the demolition? I thought you could take the first sledgehammer swing."

I laughed. "Are you sure you can trust me? I've never handled one before. What if I make a mess?"

He walked with me to the back door. "Temperance, with everything you've accomplished in the last week, there isn't anything you can't do. Cracking plaster will be easy. Besides, this crew will give you an entirely new appreciation for the word *'destruction'* by the time they finish today."

I put on the bright yellow hat, adjusted it so it felt secure, and grinned. "Let's get this party started." Laughing, I said, "Oops. It's not a party. Remember the last one I held?"

Russ smiled. "Whatever you want to call it, this is a new beginning; this is your just desserts, which you deserve."

Turning slowly, I smiled, looking at my friends and neighbors who had given up their Saturday to help me. "This is a fresh start, and I baked cupcakes for everyone."

If you loved Just Desserts & Murder, help other readers find this book:

Please leave a review now!

Are you ready to read more from Temperance and the gang in Oak Hollow?

Keep reading for a sneak peek of

Cupcakes & Murder

A Temperance Matthews Cozy Mystery

A Little Bakery Cozy Mystery Series

Order Now

Or

Shop at Lucinda Race

Lucinda

I hope you want to keep up with my crazy antics of writing, gardening, cooking, and life with the pups.

Not ready to stop reading yet? If you sign up for my newsletter at www.lucindarace.com/newsletter, you will receive an excerpt for Cookies & Capers, the introduction of when Lily met Milo right away, as my thank-you gift for choosing to get my newsletter.

Cupcakes & Murder

Enjoy this humorous, small-town, psychic, cozy mystery by best-selling and award-winning author, Lucinda Race.

In Oak Hollow, every recipe comes with a dash of mystery...

After her beloved bakery goes up in flames, former FBI data analyst Temperance Matthews is determined to rise from the ashes—literally. With the support of her best friend Josie, her loyal dachshund Hank, and a budding home kitchen renovation, she's baking her way back into business in the small town of Oak Hollow.

But when one of the volunteers who helped demo her new space is found dead—

and another is discovered unconscious beside the river—after eating one of her famous chocolate cupcakes—Temperance finds herself caught in the center of a town-wide whodunit. With her sharp instincts (and an old FBI habit of connecting the dots), she starts sniffing around. Good thing her new friend, Officer Casey Butler, doesn't mind a little amateur help.

As secrets swirl to the surface and the list of suspects grows longer than a grocery receipt, Temperance must whip up the truth before someone else gets burned—and before her second chance at sweet success crumbles for good.

Cupcakes and Murder is Book 2 in the Little Bakery Cozy Mystery Series, featuring Temperance Matthews. Each book can be read as a stand alone.

📚 Fans of:

- *Jana DeLeon's Miss Fortune Series*
- *Ellie Alexander's Bakeshop Mysteries*
- *Jenn McKinlay's Cupcake Bakery Series*
- *Murder She Baked*

will fall for this emotionally rich, twist-filled cozy featuring a smart, capable heroine who knows that sometimes the sweetest confections hide the darkest secrets.

Little Bakery Cozy Mystery Series
Book Two
Cup Cakes & Murder
LUCINDA RACE

SNEEK PEEK - CUPCAKES & MURDER

Chapter 1

I stacked the last five boxes of cupcakes on the folding table next to the sidewalk—four to a box, each one frosted and ready to taste. Josie ran up and handed me a sign that read, FREE! *Thanks for helping on demo day.*

With a chuckle, I said, "Nice touch. All you needed to add was: new location of Early Rise Two."

With a grin, she whipped out a sign from behind her back. "I'm one step ahead of you, Temperance. It's time people knew what's next for the bakery. Besides, giving out cupcakes is the perfect way to share the news."

"I put a list of ingredients on the box too in case someone has an allergy to any items I used to bake them."

Josie sank down on the wide porch steps of the Victorian home I inherited from my Aunt Penny. She said, "My feet ache and I'm exhausted. Now that everyone's gone we should sit for a few minutes. Oh, and I called in for a pizza and salad delivery."

I glanced at the large roll-off dumpster in my driveway with mountains of debris. It was the remnants from the housekeeper's apartment at the back of my home. "This might be a trend with you being one step ahead of me." I waved to Officer Casey Butler as she strode up the walk. We'd become well acquainted last week during the arson investigation when my bakery was reduced to ash and rubble.

"Casey, care for a cupcake?"

She perused the table. "I don't need four decadent little treats."

I waved. "Take a box. They'll keep for a few days. Just store them in the refrigerator in the box."

"In that case, I don't mind if I do." She picked up a box and crossed to where we sat. "How did today go?"

"Better than I ever expected. Russ Patterson enlisted about twenty volunteers, most of whom were subcontractors he uses. Erik Wool, Van Jonas, and Dave Buckle came to provide any first aid should it be needed. And if that wasn't enough, Renee Santorini from Sassy's Slice made party-size subs for everyone at lunch."

Josie said, "Don't forget Belle Green sent over people from the brewery to help out this morning."

"I'm sorry I missed it." Casey sat on a lower step. "With all that help it must have made short work out of clearing the apartment." Her gaze slid from one side of my yard to the other. "Where's all the stuff?"

Clasping my hands behind my head, I exhaled. "Most of it was gone as fast as it was carried to the curb. What was left, a man named Jonesy stopped by and asked if he could have the rest. He has a third-hand store in Pine Valley, so I told him to have at it."

Casey's brow knitted together. "What's a third-hand store?"

I smiled. "He explained it like this—said since the curb scoopers gave stuff a second life after tag sales, anything overlooked was third-hand. It's an interesting take on household goods, don't you think?"

"Sure. At least you don't need to have anyone haul away what was left," she said.

Josie asked, "Casey, do you want to stay for an early dinner? I ordered pizza and salad."

"That sounds great. I'm off duty tonight."

"Ha, from what we've seen in the last week, you're never really off duty."

She grinned. "Sleep is overrated."

"There was a scuffle today. Josie, did you happen to overhear what set off Franny and Gloria?"

"Well, Gloria grabbed Franny's arm, and Jacob and Chase stepped in to pull them apart. I'm not sure what the argument was about, but the good thing is the four of them left soon after lunch and in different directions."

Casey asked, "I don't think I know them. Are they local?"

Josie replied, "Chase Clark is Franny's brother, and a landscaping company employs him and Gloria that Kelly Woods owns which is an extension of Twigs and Petal Garden Center. You might have seen the trucks around; the logo is T&P. Franny works at the garden center. Jacob's a mechanic at Stu's Garage. To get back to the tussle, I'm clueless about the ladies' argument. I've never witnessed Gloria that angry. Typically, she's mild-mannered."

"I hope they work everything out." A couple of kids on bikes zipped down the street, did a U-turn at the end, and slowly crept by, ogling the cupcakes. "Take a box," I called out.

The one boy wearing a baseball cap said, "My mom said I needed to ask permission first."

"You have permission to take a box of cupcakes as long as you like chocolate."

He nodded and looked at his buddy. "Want some?"

The other boy grinned. "Heck yeah."

Thanks, Ms. Matthews." The ball cap boy waved and took the box. "See ya."

"He knew my name; too bad I didn't know his."

"That's Kennedy Moore's son, Billy; he's got good manners. The other boy is Jeff Collins."

"Right, Kennedy owns My Closet. I haven't done much shopping since moving to town but she's got nice window displays."

Josie stood. "Temperance, your exhausted. I'll get plates and silverware and we can sit on the porch for dinner."

I stretched my arms overhead. "No, let's eat on the deck. My little doxie needs to stretch his legs. Hank's been good but he's had a boring day being stuck in my office and I don't want him up all night looking to play. Besides, with just a few boxes of cupcakes left maybe they'll go quicker if we aren't hovering."

"I can pick up pizza," Casey said.

"Delivery tonight. We were too tired." I opened the door and ushered Josie and Casey inside. Taking one last look at the boxes of cakes, I smiled. It had been a great day.

A toot of a horn drew my attention to the driveway—a small blue hatchback parked with its engine running. A pizza slice on the roof confirmed dinner had arrived.

"I'll be right in. Dinner's here." I jogged down the steps. "Hey, Gordon." It was ironic he was the pizza delivery guy. He was so thin, it looked like he could eat one a day and still look like a reed.

"Hi Temperance," he pushed a button, the hatch on his car opened, and he got out. "I've got your dinner right here."

"Great, we're starving."

He took in the dumpster. "I heard you're going to reopen your bakery. That's a good thing. It's real popular around town."

"On a smaller scale, and it won't be for a couple of months. We finished the demo today on the apartment at the back of the house. Hence the dumpster."

"My sister, Gloria, and her friends, Franny, Jacob, and

Chase, were supposed to help." His gaze slid to the boxes of cupcakes, and he licked his lips. "Are you selling those?"

"Your sister and her friends did a fantastic job, and the cupcakes are free. Would you like a box?"

"Yes, please."

He took a pizza box and a large paper bag out of the back and closed the hatch, following me to the steps. "Order was paid for and tip included too. But I will grab a box as an added bonus," he grinned.

I took our dinner order. "Help yourself."

"Thanks, and I'm glad to hear you're not letting a little setback derail you."

I smiled. "Never. Have a great night and enjoy the cupcakes."

"We will." He picked up a box and yelled, "Thanks again." He paused before getting in the car. "You know, I could give a box to Henrietta Woods; she can write a piece for the Oak Hollow Gazette just to let folks know you're a phoenix. She's having dinner with friends at Sassy's. I could give her a box if you'd like."

A little publicity wouldn't hurt. "Sure, take all three boxes, and if you see anyone else you want to give one to, go for it."

"Will do." His long strides ate up the lawn between him and the card table. He nodded as he picked up the remaining three boxes of cakes and beamed. "Yeah. Temperance Matthews, the phoenix. I like it."

"Thanks again, Gordon."

He set the boxes on the passenger seat and backed out of the drive.

"Well, that's the last of them."

Josie held the door for me. "What was that all about?"

I climbed the steps and went to the kitchen. "You'll laugh. Gordon called me a phoenix, and I gave him the last of the cupcakes to pass out. He said Henrietta might do a write-up on the new venture. It's a great idea to let people know what's happening with the little bakery."

Casey held Hank on her lap when we entered the kitchen. "Are you laughing after all you've accomplished today? What are you, a superhero?"

I shook my head. "Gordon Nardin delivered our dinner, and he took the last of the cupcakes to pass out to his friends. Before he left, he said I was a phoenix."

With a grin, she put Hank on the floor. "I'll second that. I've never seen anyone take adversity and turn it around as fast. It's great to see the town rally around you."

"It feels good to know I'm an accepted part of the community." I tapped the center of my chest.

Josie took the bag, which contained the salad. "You had doubts?"

"I'm an outsider. Most people in town, you included, are generations deep. My aunt lived here and I was a summer resident. It's not quite the same."

Casey nodded. "I get it. I grew up in the mid-west, but Oak Hollow residents are pretty welcoming. I'm glad I made the move."

I nodded. Before I could speak my stomach growled so loud even Hank looked up, his ears cocked. Laughing I said, "Let's eat."

Hank barked, ran to the sliding glass door, and, bouncing on his front paws, gave another excited bark. "Someone wants to go outside."

"Is the fence repaired?" Casey asked.

Her mention of the fence caused my heart to flip in my chest, reminding me of the fire that could have taken everything from me, including my sweet pup. "Yesterday, the fence company finished fixing it. Since it only involved replacing two panels, they could fit me into the schedule. This helps with Hank since he hates to be on a leash, and he's a dog built around a nose. If someone were grilling hotdogs in Asheville, he'd be gone like a flash of lightning."

Josie laughed, "I've seen him in action, and Temperance isn't kidding." She clapped her hands together and slid them in opposite directions. "Greased lightning."

We sat at the round table on the deck, leaving the slider open for Hank. Despite Casey only knowing us for a few days, sitting there, it felt like we'd known each other for years.

"Temperance, are you sorry you left the FBI?" Casey sipped her beer.

Mentioning my former job didn't cause a pang of regret. "Not at all. I'm not tooting my own horn, but even if you're good at something, if it doesn't make you happy, why keep doing it? I felt like I had lost a part of my soul, and the only thing that made me happy was baking. I used to call Aunt Penny every Sunday to tell her what I had baked over the weekend. She's the one who urged me to think about making a change. When she passed away, I had just finished a heart-wrenching case, and I couldn't analyze data objectively after that."

"Do you want to talk about the case?"

I heard the empathy-filled words from Casey, and Josie's eyes were soft with unshed tears. I never shared with anyone what had happened. I wasn't about to tell my friends how I had failed.

I shook my head. "Not now." Squeezing my eyes shut to blink away the tears, I got up. "Hank, come here, little boy."

He was happily digging a crater near my veggie garden. I gave a sharp whistle, and he lifted his head, gave me a side eye, and went right back digging.

Sinking into the chair, I picked up my wine glass. "The hole doesn't matter, he's having fun. I'll fill it in later."

Casey glanced at Josie and she shrugged her shoulders.

"Who do you think Gordon is going to give the cupcakes too?"

"He mentioned the editor of the newspaper. I'm hoping Henrietta will give me a write up about the new venture and I'm sure his friends too. I'm happy they won't go to waste."

"If there were any left, I would have grabbed them to take to the station."

I slapped the table with my hand. "Dang, I should have dropped them at the fire station. That would have been good. Oh, well, tomorrow's another day that I can bake and drop something to them. Maybe I'll make bread too. They could have it with their dinner. Erik mentioned they never turn down food."

"Didn't you lose your sourdough starter?" Josie asked.

"Yes, but I'll make a new starter, and by the time I'm baking again for sales, it will be strong."

Casey bobbed her head. "Gordon was right, calling you a phoenix. I don't think there isn't anything you can't overcome."

"Well, the symbolism of rising from the ashes isn't lost on me, but I'd rather have a different metaphor since I've had two fires within two days. However, only good days are ahead of me now. I picked up my slice of pizza and grinned. "I can feel it in my bones."

Josie held up her wine glass. "We should toast to that."

Casey lifted her bottle, and I did the same with my glass. We tapped them together. "Here's to analyzing the taste of my baked goods and not crime scene data."

Josie said, "To your future baking endeavors."

Casey grinned, "And this cop loves all baked goods, not just donuts."

I laughed. "I'll keep that in mind, Officer."

Order Now

To keep reading what happens next with Temperance and the gang in Oak Hollow.

A FREE STORY FOR YOU

Have you enjoyed Just Desserts & Murder? Not ready to stop reading yet? If you sign up for my newsletter at www.lucin darace.com/newsletter, you will receive Cookies & Capers, which is the start of Lily and Milo's adventure, as my thank-you gift for choosing to get my newsletter.

Cookies & Capers

I stood in front of the old wood and glass door as I pocketed the keys to the Cozy Nook Bookshop. Aunt Mimi had signed her bookstore over to me. She said it felt like giving me her baby. But I loved the shop as much as my aunt did. We had worked together for the last twelve years. After attending the University of Maine, I had a degree in history and education. I had always wanted to be a teacher, but jobs were scarce and after substituting for a few years, I moved back to my hometown of Pembroke, Maine, and Aunt Mimi hired me as soon as I unpacked my suitcase.

Spending time with my aunt, learning the business, had

been the best experience. I offered to buy the shop when she wanted to retire, but she wouldn't hear of it. As long as she had free books for life, and her long-term boyfriend Nate, she said it was a fair deal. From my point of view, I had built-in backup for years to come.

Now that I was the bookshop owner, Aunt Mimi was no longer coming in every day which meant her cat, Phoenix, wasn't either and the space felt empty without a kitty lying in the window or skulking about as kitties do. I was off to the Pembroke Animal Palace to see if I could find a match.

It was a short walk in the bright noonday sun. The spring air from the ocean carried a tang of salt, but the breeze was refreshing. I waved to one of my best friends, Gage Erikson, as he drove past in his police-issued sedan. My heart fluttered in my chest.

He was a detective on the force. Not that we had much crime in our small seaside town. But one of these days I was going to get brave and tell him I had been carrying a torch for him since we were in ninth grade. What's the worst thing that could happen? We'd still be best friends, right?

I continued down the brick sidewalk, waving to William North from the Sweet Spot Bakery. He was sweeping the area around the small bistro tables in front of the bakery. William was wearing a large pristine white apron and a wide smile. A deep inhale confirmed my suspicion. He was baking cookies. My mouth watered. I did a half turn and went back to where he was finishing up. "Good morning, William." I bobbed my head in the shop's direction. "What is that tantalizing smell?"

He held open the brightly polished glass door. "One of your favorites, Lily. Chocolate chip and pecan cookies. Can I interest you in one before you continue on your mission?"

I gave him a side-look. "Mission?"

He chuckled. "Over the years my Lulu had said you had two speeds, strolling and purposeful. Just now it was purposeful so hence you're on a mission."

"I'm going to the shelter, hoping to find a kitty. The shop is lonely now that Phoenix is home every day with Aunt Mimi, and I think a cat napping in the window adds an air of serenity to the place."

"Unless you're allergic."

He had a point, but I was not willing to be deterred. I smiled. "I'm always happy to deliver to a customer." I leaned over the glass bakery case, like a kid pressing her nose against the candy case. "You made sugar cookies too and frosted them?" I sighed. I was going to need to exercise more if he continued to bake all my favorites. He was smiling at me as I looked up. "Are the chocolate pecan ready?"

He wiggled his eyebrows. "I have a tray cooling in the back."

"Then can I have one of those and a sugar cookie, but to go?"

With a flick of his wrist, he snapped open a white bakery bag and called over his shoulder. "Jerilyn, would you please bring out the last batch of cookies?"

I heard a muffled, coming, and smiled. "It's good that Jerilyn stayed on." I said nothing about his beloved wife Lulu. Rumor had it she was ill and not doing well.

He nodded. "It is. She's a hard worker and excellent with the customers."

Jerilyn bustled in from the back room carrying a large stainless-steel tray. It was lined with parchment paper and cookies the size of the palm of my hand. It was going to taste so good with a hot cup of tea later.

William put two in the bag, along with two sugar cookies, and then he handed it to me. I paid for my cookies and thanked him. "Stop by the shop later. You might just get to meet my new fur baby."

"Sounds like a plan." He grinned and crossed his arms over his rounded midsection. "You're more like your aunt than you realize. Ever since she opened that bookshop, she's had a cat, too."

I paused, tucked the bakery bag in my tote, and with my hand on the door, I turned and gave him a wide grin. "And now it's time I carry on the tradition." With a jaunty wave, I called, "Wish me luck."

Cookies & Capers is only available by signing up for my newsletter – sign up for it here at www.lucindarace.com/newsletter

LOVE TO READ?

All ebooks and paperback copies can be ordered from my website at:
Shop at Lucinda Race

Cozy Mystery Books
A Bookstore Cozy Mystery Series
Books & Bribes
It was an ordinary day until the book of Practical Magic conked Lily on the head causing her to see stars. And then she discovered her cat, Milo, could talk.

Catnaps & Crimes
The fun continues as Lily practices her magic and needs to investigate another murder.

Tea & Trouble
A fall festival, reading tea leaves and a few clues propel Lily into a new murder investigation.

Scares & Dares

Love to Read?

What goes wrong at a haunted house is anything but expected until Lily starts following the clues.

Holidays & Homicide
Can Lily solve a murder before it ruins the holidays?

Leprechauns & Larceny
Will a dead leprechaun take the shine off the wedding?

Magicians & Murder
When four magicians roll into town for a show more than fun is on one person's mind.

Artifacts & Amulets
Milo has been keeping secrets, which can be deadly.

Cranberries & Criminals November 2024
Whose half-baked idea was it for bookstore owner and witch Lily Michaels to enter an amateur baking contest in her small town of Pembroke Cove, Maine?

Broomsticks & Blooms
The time has come for Lily to learn to fly.

Fishing & Forgery April 2025
A simple Sunday fishing adventure with friends where Lily and her friends reel in the big one.

Wands & Weddings May 2025
Lily and Gage are ready to tie the knot. But what's up with the coven's council? Can Lily unravel this new mystery before she says, I do.
Inheritance & illusions 2026
Pages & Potions
Legacy & Lies

Ghostly Gowns Series
A Paranormal Ghost Cozy Mystery Series
Ghost and Gowns
Buttons & Burglary
Pleats & Poison
Ribbons & Robbery

Cowboys of River Junction
Second Chances in Montana
Twenty years later, Renee and Hank are back where they fell in love, but reality is like a spring frost, and is a long-distance relationship their only option for their second chance?

Stars Over Montana
The cowboy broke her heart, but he never stopped loving her. Now, she's back ready to run her grandfather's ranch…

Hiding in Montana
Can love flourish while danger lurks in the shadows?

Moonlight Over Montana
From the smoldering ash, she realizes he's all the family she and her daughter need.

The Sandy Bay Series
<u>Sundaes on Sunday</u>
A widowed school teacher and the airline pilot whose little girl is determined to bring her daddy and the lady from the ice cream shop together for a second chance at love.

Last Man Standing/Always a Bridesmaid
Barrett
Has the last man standing finally met his match?

Marie

Love to Read?

Career-focused city girl discovers small town charm can lead to love.

Price Family Romance Series
Breathe
Her dream come true may be the end of his...
Crush
The first time they met was fleeting; the second time restarted her heart.
<u>Blush</u>
He's always loved her but he left and now he's back…the question, does she still love him?
Vintage
He's an unexpected distraction, she gets his engine running…
<u>Bouquet</u>
Sweet second chances for a widow and the handsome billionaire...

Last Chance Beach
Shamrocks are a Girl's Best Friend
Will a bit of Irish luck and a matchmaking uncle give Kelly and Tric a chance to find love?

A Holiday Romance
Holiday Heart Wishes
Heartfelt wishes and holiday kisses…

<u>Holiday Heart Wishes</u>
Hockey, holidays, and a slap shot to the heart.

<u>Christmas in July</u>
She's the hometown girl with the hometown advantage. Right?

<u>A Secret Santa Christmas</u>
Christmas just isn't Holly's thing, but will a family secret help her find the true meaning of Christmas?
The Sugar Plum Inn

The chef and the restaurant critic are about to come face to face.
Holiday Romance Box Set
Sweet with a touch of heat holiday romance novels.

It's Just Coffee Series
The Matchmaker and The Marine
She vowed never to love again. His career in the Marines crushed his ability to love. Can undeniable chemistry and a leap of faith overcome their past?

The MacLellan Sisters Trilogy
Old and New
An enchanted heirloom wedding dress and a letter change three sisters' lives forever as they fulfill their grandmother's last request to try on the dress.
Borrowed
He's just a borrowed boyfriend. He might also be her true love.
Blue
Will an enchanted wedding dress work its magic one more time?

McKenna Family Romance Series

Lost and Found
Love never ends... A widow who talks to her late husband and her handsome single neighbor who has secretly loved her for years.
The Journey Home
Where do you go to heal your heart? You make the journey home...
The Last First Kiss
When life handed Kate lemons, she baked.
Ready to Soar
Kate will fight for love, won't she?
Love in the Looking Glass
Will Ellie's first love be her last or will she become a ghost like her father?
Magic in the Rain

Dani's plan of hiding in plain sight may not have been the best idea.
After All These Years
February 2025
Arielle Clark is a famous artist with a painful past. When her first love comes to town, ghosts from the past are resurrected. But can the embers of love still linger after all these years?

SOCIAL MEDIA

Follow Me on Social Media

Like my Facebook page
Join Lucinda's Heart Racer's Reader Group on Facebook
Twitter @lucindarace
Instagram @lucindaraceauthor
BookBub
Goodreads
Pinterest
YouTube

ABOUT THE AUTHOR

Award-winning and best-selling author Lucinda Race is an avid fan of fiction. As a young girl, she spent hours reading cozy mystery and romance novels, getting lost in the fun and hope they represented. While her friends dreamed of becoming doctors and engineers, she dreamed of becoming an expert at crafting captivating novels.

As life twisted and turned, she wrote nonfiction but longed to return to her true passion. After developing the storylines for the McKenna Family Romance series and the Paranormal Cozy Nook Bookstore Series, she decided to start living her dream. Her fingers practically fly over computer keys. She weaves paranormal cozy mystery stories and romance with guaranteed happily ever afters.

Lucinda lives with her two little dogs, a miniature long-haired dachshund and a shitzu mix rescue, in the rolling hills of western Massachusetts. She's immersed in her fictional worlds, writing mystery, suspense, and romance novels or reading everything she can get her hands on.